THE PHILOSOPHER STORIES

ESSENTIAL PROSE SERIES 217

Canada Council for the Arts   **Conseil des Arts du Canada**

ONTARIO ARTS COUNCIL
CONSEIL DES ARTS DE L'ONTARIO
an Ontario government agency
un organisme du gouvernement de l'Ontario

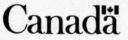
Canadä

Guernica Editions Inc. acknowledges the support of the Canada Council for the Arts and the Ontario Arts Council. The Ontario Arts Council is an agency of the Government of Ontario.

We acknowledge the financial support of the Government of Canada.

THE PHILOSOPHER STORIES

JERRY LEVY

GUERNICA
EDITIONS
TORONTO · CHICAGO · BUFFALO · LANCASTER (U.K.)
2024

Guernica Founder: Antonio D'Alfonso

Michael Mirolla, general editor
Julie Roorda, editor
David Moratto, interior and cover design

Guernica Editions Inc.
1241 Marble Rock Rd., Gananoque, ON K7G 2V4
2250 Military Road, Tonawanda, N.Y. 14150-6000 U.S.A.
www.guernicaeditions.com

Distributors:
Independent Publishers Group (IPG)
600 North Pulaski Road, Chicago IL 60624
University of Toronto Press Distribution (UTP)
5201 Dufferin Street, Toronto (ON), Canada M3H 5T8

First edition.
Printed in Canada.

Legal Deposit—First Quarter
Library of Congress Catalog Card Number: 2023949805
Library and Archives Canada Cataloguing in Publication
Title: The philosopher stories / Jerry Levy.
Names: Levy, Jerry, author.
Series: Essential prose series ; 217.
Description: First edition. | Series statement: Essential prose series ; 217
Identifiers: Canadiana (print) 20230562132 |
Canadiana (ebook) 20230562140 | ISBN 9781771838757 (softcover) |
ISBN 9781771838764 (EPUB)
Subjects: LCGFT: Short stories.
Classification: LCC PS8623.E959 P55 2024 | DDC C813/.6—dc23

"We are all in the gutter,
but some of us are looking at the stars."
—OSCAR WILDE

CONTENTS

PRELUDE . . . . *ix*

FAMILY LIFE *1*
ONE PUNCH *21*
THE STORY THIEF *33*
THE HOVEL *57*
THE BOOK SALE *69*
THE TRUTH SEEKER *79*
REJECTION *93*
EDNA *115*
EASY COME, EASY GO *131*
THE LOVER *147*
WHEN SHE LEFT *185*
BROKEN DREAMS *205*

ACKNOWLEDGEMENTS *219*
ABOUT THE AUTHOR *221*

PRELUDE

Once, in a small, nondescript apartment above a butcher shop in the heart of Toronto's Kensington Market, there lived a philosopher of sorts, a failed philosopher by most accounts. But for the most part, he didn't think of himself that way; in fact, he considered himself a *superman*, the *Übermensch* modelled after the 19th century German philosopher Friedrich Nietzsche's treatise. Could he leap over tall buildings? Was he faster than a speeding bullet? No, it wasn't like that. Our man in the Market couldn't do any of those things. Ah, but morally, that was different. He believed that maybe, just maybe, if all the perfect pieces fell into place, he would be able to save the world, advance mankind by unlocking the unenlightened shackles that constricted it. That were rotting it. It was a tall order to be certain, but our philosopher believed he could be a great man, an influential man, and escape from the ugliness of life … especially if those pieces fell right into his lap, manna from the heavens. As it turned out, other things came his way, highly unusual things that he wasn't in the least expecting. And, if truth be told, sometimes the philosopher thought he was only fooling himself with his grandiose dreams. Secretly, he seemed to know better.

These are the philosopher's stories.

FAMILY LIFE

My parents were *Roma* from Hungary, *gypsies* as some people like to say. *Thieves* and *witches* yet to others. They were heavily persecuted and fled to Canada, but that perpetual outcast label remained etched in their psyches, an attitude they passed on to me. I was the outsider throughout school, never making any friends. It was my parents and me against the world. Sure, they settled into jobs in Toronto and tried to fit in, a little anyway. They were smart people, somewhat educated, but the jobs they got here were menial cleaning ones in office buildings, bringing only the basics of food to the table and shelter over our heads. We could afford no luxuries of any sort, had no car, and certainly there were no trips. Even taking public transit wasn't feasible —I rode my rickety bicycle everywhere, even in the winter. My nose froze, my hands froze, my feet too; it didn't matter though, there was no choice. Besides, once my dad showed me how to patch a flat tire, I felt a sense of autonomy ... nothing could get the better of me if I needed to be somewhere.

I suppose things might have been different if my parents had reached out to the various Canadian social service agencies set up to help refugees, but that didn't happen. They had an innate distrust of institutions and regarded any such governmental agency as a thing to be avoided, just like in Hungary where the government often perpetrated violence against the Roma people. Like I said, my parents were pretty sharp but they just couldn't shake that innate distrust of certain things. Corporations.

As might be expected, my parents argued constantly about money. With her old-world views, my mother believed that, as the man of the house, my father should be the one to keep the family in comfort. But with no real skills to offer and with language an issue, especially at first, he was at a vocational dead-end. Much to his credit though, he, just like my mother, mastered the English language particularly well in time. Still, it wasn't enough.

It didn't help matters that we lived in Parkdale at the time. It was becoming more gentrified each year, with young urban families and professionals buying and restoring some of the grand old houses. New shops and cafés began opening on King Street and some of the parks were being swept clean of vagrants. Amidst all this change were my very guarded parents. They were without means, and while my father seemed to not be bothered in the least by the opulence that was springing up around him, my mother was a different story. She would gaze wistfully into the windows of pricey dress shops or else deliberately take walks by the refurbished Victorian houses, with their prim gardens and terraced brick exteriors. On occasion, she would even dare to walk up to the front door and spy through the windows. I know this because she often reported to both my father and me about what she saw inside—magnificent chandeliers, spacious living rooms with leather furniture, accent tables, curio cabinets, pine bookcases. It ate at her, being so close to such luxury, and yet so far. My father begged her to stop but she would hear none of it, satisfying her desires temporarily by buying a blouse or dress or a pair of shoes that was beyond our means. Sometimes she even stole the flowers that dotted the lawns of the homes she so coveted.

***

I never expected to be happy. Growing up, I never knew what that was. I have often thought that life would be easier, happier, if I were, well, more normal. But I'm not. Never have been. I've always felt on edge, teetering somewhere between reality and illusion, a complete outsider not only to others, but to myself as well. I always wanted to fit in. But even as a child. I just didn't know how. I turned others off. Maybe it was because I didn't talk a lot. I could talk, but I avoided doing so. *Selective Mutism*, that's what I now call it. Because I didn't have a lot to say. Because people sometimes annoyed me.

So I play-acted and pretended to be someone else, just to fit in. I made up a whole personality profile for myself, different from my true nature. I figured that might help. I said I was from the star system Pleiades. A magical and faraway place. You know the one, it's in the constellation Taurus, precisely 432.7582 light years from Earth. (Scientists aren't exactly sure of the distance and often simply say "430 light years". That disturbs me, how imprecise they are, so I devised my own mathematical formula to calculate the distance. A very complicated one that, even to this day, I keep to myself.)

At home, I knew that my parents would never believe I was an alien. After all, my mom gave birth to me right in Toronto. That's not in the Pleiades. Not even close. So I never mentioned it to them. But in the outside world, away from home, well, that's where I used my alternate personality. Kind of like Clark Kent turning into Superman. Or Bruce Wayne into Batman. Peter Parker morphing into Spiderman. *Morphing*, I like that word. You get the idea though. Alter-egos seemed to work just fine for them, so I figured it would come in handy for me.

Unfortunately, I couldn't keep my secret from my parents. It came out all the same. First from teachers, then from children's parents, children that I tried (unsuccessfully) to befriend. In Grade 5, Ms. Atkinson, my teacher, called my mom in for an interview. (My father never went to these type of school events for some reason, but it wasn't a problem for her as she knew the schools were on our side.)

"Do you know your son is saying he's from the Pleiades?" Ms. Atkinson said.

My mom didn't know anything about astronomy. But she always stood up for me, no matter what.

"He reads a lot of comic books," my mom said. "So I'm not surprised. He got it from there, I'm sure. You know how children are, wanting to be exactly like their superheroes. Where is this Pleiades anyway?"

"It's a star system very, very far away. But the point is that Karl is insistent. He has very precise information about this otherworldly place. He tells his classmates that the Pleiades are sometimes called the Seven Sisters. And it all has to do with Greek mythology; according to him, the Pleiades were the seven daughters of Atlas, a God who held up the sky, and his wife who was a protector of sailing. My word, he even knows the names of the daughters!"

"Ok, I'll talk to him about that. But what about his grades, how he's generally doing in school?"

"Oh, no problems there. Karl is incredibly smart as you can see from his incredible knowledge of mythology and the star system. Really, really bright."

So that was that. I would never have known about being ratted out by the teacher if my mom hadn't sat me down after the interview and told me everything that was said. She also asked me if it were true that I go around telling other children that I'm from the Pleiades. So I had to confess.

"I did research," I told her. "On the 'net. Comic books talk about it too. It wasn't hard to find."

"Ok, but son. The question is: *why are you saying this?* You don't actually believe you're from the Pleiades, do you? Do you?"

"I can't be Paul McCartney for you," I said, "because I have no rhythm. It's impossible for me to sing. *Yah! Yah! Boom shaka-lakka.*" I waved my arms around maniacally. "You see, no rhythm."

"Oh my goodness."

"But maybe I can be from the Pleiades."

"Oh my goodness," my mother reiterated, shaking her head.

I shrugged my shoulders, and my mom accepted what I had said. And the McCartney business touched her heart because I knew he was her favourite singer. After our little talk, the matter was dropped. She never brought it up again, not even when other parents contacted her about the very same thing, their children complaining how weird I was, how I told amazing stories about this far-off galaxy where I had spent my first few years. But I think she got it, why I told everyone I was from another star system. It had nothing to do with McCartney. It was all about compensating. Compensating for being *different*. That's what I gathered, what I now surmise in my adult years.

Unfortunately, for the most part, pretending I was from out of this world didn't help me win new friends. I would tell other children that I had no problem flying on my home planet. But that it didn't work so well on earth, mostly because gravity was too strong here.

***

My mom was right. I did read a lot of comic books growing up. And yes, she was also right that I took my Pleiadian alter-ego from those very pages. But it wasn't only comic books that I read. Well, at first, it was comics. But later on I read all sorts of books. I just loved reading. There was nothing like it. I didn't have any real friends so books became my constant companions. Oh, I actually did have one constant friend. Natasha, my personal assistant, the one I programmed into my PC. An ingenious piece of software, especially for a kid. I could type questions to her and she would answer. Better yet, owing to Windows voice recognition, I could speak to Natasha and she would talk back. A true friend. I would spend hour upon hour talking to her. Natasha had an endless store of information, was very patient, and didn't mind when I asked the same question over and over again, as I liked to do. On the weekends especially, when there was no school, I would hide in my room, chat with Natasha, and only come out for meals. She even knew my alter-ego name. That conversation went like this:

Natasha: "What can I help you with?"

Me: "Natasha, do you know my name?"

Natasha: "Your name is Karl. But because we're good friends, I can call you *Zazie*, your Pleiadian name."

Zazie: "Natasha, do you know why I came to this Earth?"

Natasha: "I have no particular insights into the motivations of Pleiadians, Zazie."

Zazie: "Natasha, who is my best friend?"

Natasha: "You have no other friends, you have told me many times. So by extension I am your only friend and your best friend. Now can we get back to work, Zazie?"

That's exactly what I liked about Natasha. The no-nonsense approach, ready to do work. And we did a lot of that together, all the time. I would ask Natasha many questions about technology, math, science, literature, and many, many other topics, and I'd get answers. Sometimes, although not very often, Natasha didn't have the answers and readily admitted as much. That too was fine. I appreciated the honesty. It only meant we had to try harder.

* * *

Growing up, my mother was my whole world. My father too but I gravitated more toward her, maybe because he was away working so much. So I learned to like whatever she did. Anything. She was a big Paul McCartney fan as I've mentioned and she'd make me sit and watch his videos, especially the ones where he appeared in concert, like the Concert for Diana at Wembley Stadium. People were singing along and dancing throughout the concerts, but I didn't get it, I wasn't into music. But my mom tried to sway me, saying that her idol had a certain energy on stage, he was free-flowing, a musical genius. Whatever. She also told me that she loved his songs (and knew all the words), his youthful appearance, dance moves, all of it. Mostly she loved his voice. She said that, if mankind had to invent a pure rock 'n roll voice, it would have to be his. She called it "silky smooth." I'm not sure I understood exactly what she meant by that because well, I was only eleven years old when she told me. She was my mom, so I believed her. And although I had no natural affinity for music, no talent for it, and was very "stiff" in my nature, because I loved my mom so much, I wanted to be Paul McCartney ... just for her.

***

In high school. I didn't have any friends. Well, that's not quite true. I had one—Martin Cameron. Sometimes it just seemed like I didn't have any. But Martin was a lot like me actually, preferring the company of his computer or his dog Bear to other teenagers. Bear followed Martin everywhere. They were inseparable. Bear was very big, all black, and had a very bad limp from when he was hit by a car when Martin was much younger. He had plates and screws in his right leg and they would stay there the rest of his life. But he got around just fine although he could no longer run very fast; if he did chase something, like a ball that Martin threw, he kind of hobbled quickly. Martin loved Bear and I'm sure Bear loved him.

Martin and I would eat together in the school cafeteria almost every day. Just the two of us. Martin ordered whatever was the daily special and I ordered mac 'n' cheese every day.

"You like that a lot," he said to me one day as we sat opposite each other and read our comic books.

"You mean this comic book?" I felt his question was rather vague.

"No, I mean the mac 'n' cheese."

"I do. That's why I eat it."

"Did you ever think of trying something else? Meat lasagna is very good and so is the grilled cheese."

"Well, I like mac 'n' cheese. It's tasty and so I see no reason to change from that. If I ordered something else, I might not like it as much. So why take a chance? There's no reason. And reasoning makes the world go round as far as I'm concerned."

Martin shook his head very slowly. I suspected he didn't like that answer because he continued pestering me about my food choices. Once he even held out a spoonful of the beef lasagna for me to eat but I just shut my mouth tight and turned my head sideways. That was the closest Martin and I ever came to an argument. Most of the time, we got along just fine.

But aside from when we were in school, Martin and I didn't see each other all that much. I kind of missed him when he wasn't around, but again, the lure of my mom and Natasha and assorted computer games and comic books was too strong. As for Martin, I think he was shy and liked to stay in his own house on weekends anyway. Like me, he was just awkward around people, unable to meet their eyes. He was always looking down when he spoke. I never asked him about all that but, suspect that it had to do with a brown and purple stain he had below his left eye. He was born that way and it wasn't very nice to look at. But it never bothered me. I cared more that he was smart and just like me, had skipped a grade, from Grade 8 to Grade 10. When we did meet, we talked computers and science. We were both really interested in science, and often pondered the universe. How it got started, black holes, quarks, the Big Bang Theory, exoplanets ... and so on. We loved discussing NASA's Parker Solar Probe. How it was the fastest man-made object ever conceived, travelling at 672,000 km/hour, The fact it was to use the gravity of Venus to slingshot it to the sun where it would collect data on solar winds. All of this talk spurred us to consider that one day we might become astronauts. I never told Martin I was from the Pleiades star system though; there was no need.

Speaking of science, the Physics and Astronomy Department at the university held Astronomy Public Nights at the observatory. They were called Astro Tours and were free events open to the public. So Martin and I went often. We loved looking at the moon and often wondered whether it had been inhabited at one point. Or whether it was hollow, an artificial construction, as I once read online.

One clear night, we were able to detect Jupiter's giant red spot. And the Orion Nebula, that cloud of dust and gas, was always clearly visible; stars within were always forming, sometimes by the hundreds. The Orion Nebula was located just a few degrees south of the Orion Belt, which was a three-star line within the constellation Orion. We used Orion's Belt as a gauge to other things within the sky. For instance, if you extended the line far upward, past a bright star called Aldebaran, there it was, the cluster of stars that was my sometimes home, the Pleiades, 432.7582 light years from Earth. Staff at the observatory guided the public around, but left me and Martin alone to do our own thing. We had been there so often and queried them about so many things most people would not have had a clue about, that they just knew.

On occasion we would trade comic books. That too was enjoyable, but only if Martin had one that I needed. Which actually wasn't very often. Martin liked to read Richie Rich and Dennis the Menace and I thought they were totally lame compared to Superman and Spiderman. I never said anything to him but often wondered why he had such poor taste.

What I liked most about being with Martin though was that sometimes we did not speak. We would just walk down the street, him looking down at the ground with Bear at his side and me looking up at the sky. It was comfortable that way, and there was no need to say anything. Bear couldn't speak English so we made a perfect trio.

One day though Martin did start talking and it was a very uncomfortable experience.

"My parents want me to have plastic surgery," he said. "It's for my face. I don't know if you've noticed but I have a mark on it."

I had no context for this and only shrugged my shoulders.

"They say that it will help my confidence," he said. "And by doing that, I'll be in a better position in life. Like I'll be able to get a job, maybe get married. Stuff like that. That's what they say."

I wanted to tell Martin about the latest Green Lantern comic book I bought. How Green Lantern fights off a villain called Mongul. I wanted to change the subject because I couldn't figure out what to say to Martin about his parents' wish to alter his face. Of course the mark he had wasn't that nice to look at, but to be honest, if I wasn't bothered by it, why should anyone else be? And this whole business of getting married and finding a job, that was all very foreign to me. I didn't want to think about such things because that was for grown-ups … and I was very far away from that time in my life. It also made me very scared to ponder, because as far as I was concerned, I would just live with my mom the rest of my life. That was my hope anyway. I wasn't in the way at home so why would I have to get a job and get married?

So I told Martin all about Mongul and I brought up another superhero that I was very fond of, Aquaman. "You see, Martin," I said, "the comic book I just got is in a storyline associated with the Justice League of America. There's an invasion of Earth by an alien race and Aquaman is made leader because many prominent members of the League are missing. So it's a depleted group and Aquaman decides to train four new members —Gypsy, Vibe, Vixen, and Steel. It's a very good plot."

I knew Martin didn't know anything at all about Aquaman because, like I said, he was really into silly childish characters like Richie Rich and even Archie. But I figured my diversionary conversation about a superhero he knew nothing about would conveniently get me off the hook. It did, and we walked the rest of the way in silence until we got to his home. There, while looking at his shoes, he said to me: "I wish I could time travel."

That was interesting and I asked him why.

"Because then I can go back in time and make sure I was never born."

I bent down to scratch Bear under his neck. That was his favourite thing in the world ... right under the neck; he would close his eyes and seem to swoon, like he was in ecstasy. But it was then, pushing my fingers back and forth through the black fur, that I decided I was better off not being friends with Martin Cameron.

* * *

My father did the best he could but, with my mother's constant nagging and with her tendency to shop for goods we could not really afford, his heart gave out at the young age of forty-six.

Very soon after his death, my mother lost the will to live, that was evident: she was beset with crying spells, would eat only sparingly, and would often fail to show up at work. She had always been prone to bouts of self-pity—which might have explained why she felt inclined to shop at the higher end of the spectrum—and now with her husband gone, she probably realized that there was no escaping her menial life.

But she lived on. She must have realized she had to take care of me, and with the help of a few friends, she recovered. And as unlikely as it was, she even started dating again, meeting men those friends set her up with.

***

"If you always look up to superheroes, you'll never measure up. And neither will anyone else, anyone you're trying to make friends with." That was my new father talking. My stepfather. As unlikely as it seemed, my mother remarried. To a Polish man, even more of a surprise. I vaguely knew the two countries, Hungary and Poland, had always had good relations. But still, I would have thought she'd end up with another Hungarian. Maybe she should have.

When my stepfather said what he did, a lump developed in my throat and I swallowed hard. "You wouldn't say that if Batman or Superman were here with me." It was hard to believe I could come up with those words, but I did.

My stepfather looked like he was going to push me or something. He was a giant of a man, about 6'4", with broad shoulders. He had a buzzcut, like he belonged in the military or something. His big hands tightened around my shoulders and his face shrivelled up, like it was the Big Bang ready to explode. A giant cataclysm.

"Ok, show me that arm bar I taught you."

"I don't want to. I'm too old for that now."

"Show ... me ... the ... arm ... bar. If you don't show me the arm bar ..."

My stepfather lay on his back and extended his right arm in the air. I got onto my haunches on the floor next to him and held onto his forearm with both my hands. Then I maneuvered onto my backside and positioned my legs, one across his neck and the other across his waist. I squeezed my legs as tight as I could and pulled on his arm.

"Harder," he said.

"I'm doing it as hard as I can."

"Don't be a girl," he said. "What you're doing is nothing. Nothing!"

So I squeezed even harder … my legs, my hands, my arms. Eyes closed, aching with concentration, my entire body contorted into a wound-up ball. Drops of perspiration started inching down my forehead. I just imagined I was wrestling with the worst monster ever, something that came out from my closet late at night.

"Better. Now get in back of me and apply the rear-naked choke hold I taught you."

I didn't want to but I knew there was no getting out of it. So I stood up and moved to the back of my stepfather.

"No, no," he said. "Move seamlessly. Move seamlessly from the arm bar to the rear naked choke hold by swivelling on the ground. Don't stand up."

So I got back on the floor and did exactly as he said. With a heavy lump in my throat, I maneuvered from the arm bar to the choke hold.

"Choke harder."

That I didn't want to do. I was young and not especially strong, a small skinny runt compared to him, but still, I was afraid my stepfather would turn blue.

"Harder."

Then it happened. I exploded and the tears came. Like some free-flowing waterfall. I let go and stood up, bawling.

My stepfather said nothing. He looked at me as if in pity and let out a guttural sound from deep within his throat. He stood up, turned around, and walked away.

I wasn't surprised; we really didn't get along. Actually, I rarely saw him anyway; he was always away on jobs. He worked in the oil patch in Alberta. When he found out I liked comic books and was a loner, he gave up on me pretty quickly. I don't remember him teaching me anything, playing with me, nothing. Well, rasslin', if you call that *playing*. But that rasslin' bit wasn't exactly playing, in my opinion. It was more like he was trying to make me into something I was not. Or trying to break me.

* * *

There was a kid in high school called James Franklin. He had a gang around him and he was a real bully. I tried to stay as far away from him as I could. But this one day, I ran into him in the schoolyard. Or maybe he sought me out. Probably that.

"I hear you say you're from another star system," he said. "And you're called Zazie."

"Yes. No."

He turned to his posse of four other boys and laughed. Then they all laughed.

"Yes ... no? Which is it, Zazie?"

I was afraid and not sure how to answer.

"Well, I hear you've told people you're not from here," James said, "so it must be true. That means you must have superpowers then."

"No, I don't."

"Like lasers coming out of your eyes."

"No."

"Or maybe you can scale the side of a building like Spiderman."

Now for sure I didn't want to admit I was from another planet. Because if I did, I knew that James and his gang wouldn't let me leave until I showed them those powers. Actually, I didn't have to show them anything because the next thing I remembered was that I was shaken awake by a teacher, Mr. Sylvestre. He lifted me off the fence where I was hanging by my underwear. James had not only knocked me out but also given me a wedgie.

I was taken to the hospital because my lip was split open and I needed stitches. My mom met me there and started crying. She burbled something about protecting me throughout my life but that it wasn't enough, she couldn't be there all the time.

When I got home, I was only able to eat soft foods, like applesauce and Jell-O. I wasn't used to this new diet and pushed the mushy foods away at first. But then my mom told me that I would have to be on this new food for a few days. Doctor's orders. It was either eat or starve. So I ate, reluctantly.

My stepfather called when I was home. I guess my mom must have called him to let him know what happened. He asked to speak to me.

"I think he just wants to say how sorry he is about the fight," my mom said.

So I held the phone to my ear.

"Karl?"

"Yes."

"I hear you got beaten up."

I said nothing.

"Karl, arm bar. Rear-naked choke hold. How many times have I showed you how to use those to defend yourself? How many times did we practise them?" I could tell by his voice that he was upset.

I gave the phone back to my mom. Then I went to my room and applied some special ointment the doctor had recommended to my groin area because it was very red.

* * *

A number of years after their marriage, my stepfather left my mom for another woman. Just up and took off. My mom revealed to me that she didn't file for financial support for us because she didn't trust lawyers. I wasn't too happy about that, the lack of financial support. I felt my mom deserved it and it made me feel worthless for a while. A long while. Because I wondered whether I was really the cause of the non-payments.

Quite honestly, I didn't mind that my stepfather left; he was a non-factor in my life to that point anyway. And he truly didn't seem like a good fit for my mom. What I did miss though was my real father. There were things I would have liked to have done with him, with a male I could look up to. Like riding a bike, watching TV, going for car rides, discussing books, solving math problems, talking about the Hubble Telescope and its successor, the James Webb Telescope, just hanging out, those sorts of things. I had no brother (and no sister for that matter) to do these things with so it was my stepfather or no one. And it turned out to be no one.

* * *

Fairly soon after my stepfather left, my mom fell into another depression. She blamed herself for everything, the early death of my father and the premature departure of my stepfather. She considered herself an abject failure. She felt there was no point in carrying on and just before my twentieth birthday, she passed away. Natural causes, the doctors said, but I knew she had really lost the will to live.

I had started taking an interest in Philosophy at about that time and it struck me then that the Buddhists had it right when they talked about "non-attachment," the whole business of not becoming attached to anything or anyone because they eventually leave you. You can't chase happiness by becoming attached; you just enjoy it at the moment and then release it when it dissolves, when it's no longer around. I was young and not properly schooled in the tenets of certain philosophies but that's what I took from the Buddhists. At any rate, for better or worse, it ruled my life from that point on, the whole business of non-attachment. Being unseen, invisible, and alone. Unattached. Well, only attached to Philosophy. Books too.

* * *

All that was years ago. Now I live alone and the clothes that I've worn over and over again lie in piles on the floor. I scoop up the least rumpled things. Perhaps they smell, but since I'm invisible for the most part, no one cares. Not even me.

ONE PUNCH

There was a time when I studied philosophy formally, at school. The University of Toronto. I was a serious student and drawn toward the subject. I was a *thinker*, so my parents had always said. For those who embrace it, philosophy offers the opportunity of a rich inner life. A life of the mind. Where one is encouraged to examine life's larger questions in detail, to think, and to question. And lest I forget, I can say that philosophy lies within the domain of the perpetual outsider ... and I've always been an outsider, no question.

There are drawbacks, of course. For one, it really provides for no directly related employment opportunities, I always knew that. A garden-variety philosophy degree doesn't get you very far. I've heard that some lawyers have undergrad degrees in philosophy. Makes sense. After all, philosophers are analytical, logical thinkers, and can adeptly assess all angles of an argument. They're also excellent communicators. All qualities that make for a good lawyer. But I didn't care about the law. With my luck, if I had gone to law school, I'd have ended up as an "ambulance chaser" type of lawyer, appearing in ads on TV asking you to call when you were injured. Anyway, it didn't matter, this business of getting employment. I always figured I'd get by, get some sort of job that paid the bills.

Sometimes I waffled though, and considered other pursuits. Like football. Well, soccer to most North Americans. I dreamt of being a great player like Pelé or Messi, but it wasn't to be. My hand-eye co-ordination was especially bad. I just couldn't run and kick a soccer ball at the same time; I'd often trip and skin my knees. And the times I tried heading, I only succeeded in mashing up my nose. Which was all too bad because becoming a soccer player might have been a good way to get out of my own head and be involved in a more experiential life. While I have always been attracted to affairs of the mind, I had long been aware that certain things in life shouldn't be contemplated. *Just do it*, as the Nike ad says. Eating a wonderful meal, making love, romping in the ocean ... they're all better left to the senses. But in my case, I couldn't kick the damn soccer ball while I hotfooted it down the pitch, so what was I to do?

Throughout school, I supported myself with student loans and working at odd jobs—sandwich maker at Mr. Submarine, security guard at a senior's home, and dishwasher at a Chinese restaurant being amongst the least memorable. Not knowing what else to do and with my stated predilection for matters of the mind, I had fully intended to continue on with school and obtain a PhD. I knew it was a massive undertaking, but I also realized that doing so suited my nature. In writing my dissertation, I would be on my own, which, to me, would feel normal. And the end result of all my labour would be a position in academia, a professorship.

The path was charted, the route made clear by my advisor Aaron Feldstein. I had known Aaron during my undergraduate years, when he taught a course I was enrolled in called "Philosophy after 1800." Essentially a discourse on social and political currents in 19th century philosophical thought. I studied Hegel, Schopenhauer, Nietzsche, and Bertrand Russell.

Later on, I took yet another course with him entitled "The Existentialists." We delved into aspects of identity, absurdity, and alienation, and read from the works of Kierkegaard, Dostoyevsky, Tolstoy, Sartre, and Camus. Oh, and of course, Kafka. I could never forget my first reading of Kafka's *The Metamorphosis*, about the travelling salesman Gregor Samsa, who turns into a bug and stays within the confines of his room, his family understandably repulsed. A bug no less! Still, it was a very effective tool to emphasize the absurd nature of man, one locked into a world of drudgery, a world of meaningless repetition. Gregor became the manifestation of what he always was, a small and inconsequential entity.

I looked upon Aaron as a kindred spirit. He too was a loner, never quite fitting in. He was overweight, a bit of a slob (there were always food stains on his shirts), and would carry his books to school in paper shopping bags. He seemed to show little interest in women, sports, politics, fashion, movies, food, cars, business ... anything, really. Anything other than philosophy, that is. He authored many papers on diverse philosophical subjects ranging from logical empiricism to Hegelian dialectic to the Greek sophists to epistemology.

The very last course with Aaron was "The Philosophy of Law." It made sense for me to take it since I always considered, albeit half-heartedly, a career in law as a Plan B should the professorship in philosophy have failed. If truth be known, being a lawyer seemed remote for the very opposite reason that drew me toward matters of the mind, toward philosophy—one had to interact with clients in the everyday world. So while I enjoyed a certain affinity for the logic associated with the law, a career in the field did not seem overly viable. Nevertheless, as I needed a credit and given that Aaron was teaching the course, I enrolled.

For all of Aaron's accomplishments, there was one thing that stood out as being amiss: no student had ever asked him to be their advisor for the doctorate program. I was the first. In hindsight, I should have taken more heed of that fact. In *The Symposium*, Plato said that one of the highest human privileges was to "be midwife to the birth of the soul in another." Aaron never succeeded on that front. As time elapsed, I became aware that perhaps he was jealous of me, that he viewed my burgeoning academic career as threatening to his own. That was my impression. He appeared remote and provided very little in terms of mentorship. Once again I was alone. Since I believed I was too far along in the program to switch advisors and also because I viewed Aaron if not exactly as a close friend then at least an ally, I confronted him.

"I have to know your commitment level with me," I said.

"You have a persecution complex," he said without missing a beat. If there was one thing about Aaron that could not be denied, it was that he was brutally honest. "So that makes it hard for me to be there for you."

"I don't know what you mean," I said.

"It's your background. You've changed and anglicized your name from Gabor Wallachia to Karl Pringle but you still haven't shed the inferiority complex that Hungarian Romas have always exhibited. Until you do, you'll never succeed. Not only in philosophy but in anything."

It had been a long time since I had heard my birth name uttered. Not since my parents were alive. Aaron knew of my background only because I had trusted him. It now seemed as though that trust was mislaid.

Those caustic words elicited in me emotions that I had long ago suppressed—fear, anxiety, confusion, hopelessness. We continued talking, arguing, and in doing so, it became abundantly clear that Aaron wanted out of our professional relationship. He wanted to go back to being the absent-minded professor that he always was, the one without any real obligations to his students. The professor who gave lectures students complained about as being too obtuse and unrelated to the subject matter. The one who seemed to exist in his own intellectual bubble.

"There's one more thing," Aaron said.

"What's that?"

"You might want to rethink *your commitment* to the program. You've been mucking around in graduate school for six years now. Like a plague that never goes away. And you've only shown yourself to be a mediocre philosopher at best."

It was all falling apart. Rage supplanted the primary emotions of fear and terror and blinded me. I lost all control and reared back, clapping Aaron with my closed fist at the side of his head. He collapsed at once to the ground in a crumpled heap and blood spurted from his ear. For good measure, I kicked him hard in the ribs. Twice.

That one punch, of bare knuckles against pudgy flesh—which felt so good—ended my academic pursuits. I was banished from the university and made to account for my actions before a magistrate of the courts. I threw myself upon his mercy and was grateful I wasn't imprisoned. Instead, I was ordered to serve two hundred hours of community service and made to attend anger management classes. Those anger management classes eventually morphed from one-on-one sessions with a psychologist to group therapy with upwards of twenty people, many of whom had a multitude of issues like sexual abuse, gambling, alcoholism, and anger.

Despite this abomination, this descent into the bowels of the legal system from which I barely managed to escape intact, there were some positives that emerged from my pursuit of a life of the mind. For one, my years in philosophy taught me to think and to reason. And my readings in existentialism opened up doors for me into the world of literature—Camus, Dostoyevsky, Kafka, and other masters. From them I learned not only the tenets that emphasized the isolation of the individual experience in a hostile or indifferent universe, but their works also fostered in me a love for the written word. Of prose.

***

Being booted from the university forced me to look for work in the labour force. Something that I had long thought of as worthless. Work was unimportant, overrated, and able to give meaning only to those who lacked the rigorous discipline to think for themselves. An army of automatons. I would often see them debark at the St. George subway station early in the mornings, preparing to head southbound on the subway into the financial district. While I was going to the university to engage in matters of the mind, they were going to their sad and pathetic nine-to-five jobs downtown to shuffle papers, to photocopy, to take part in ridiculous conference calls, to sell their souls for money. Now, I had to join the masses and seek work opportunities that I had long eschewed. Move far from my comfort zone of sitting in parks and cafés and reading or simply observing people. Or else just wandering about the city and exploring. I'd have to get some repulsive job. I would just hold my nose and bite my tongue.

There were times though, when I just begged for money. I really wasn't cut out for working "joe-jobs" (and really, I wasn't qualified for anything else), and begging, along with scrounging about for food scraps, served me well. I began to scavenge garbage bins in back of supermarkets. "Move the bottles and cans outta the way first," one of my fellow scavengers once told me. "That way you won't step on them and end up with pieces of glass in the food. Or have your feet bleeding all over the place. That's the best system."

Lettuce, tomatoes, bread, apples, oranges, cantaloupes, avocados, celery, cheese ... I found them all. Even the occasional cob of corn. Most everything was a bit soft or brown or mouldy but I didn't mind; it was edible, that was the main thing. On one occasion I found a package of chocolate puddings, a real treat. On another, an entire case of extra-virgin olive oil, which I immediately shared with some fellow scavengers who took turns mixing it with wine, then swilling the concoction down.

The problem with dumpster-diving was that there was always lots of competition at the supermarket bins, both human and animal. Vagrants, raccoons. Most annoying of all were the "freegans," the dumpster scavengers who never failed to lecture me on the fact they were especially deserving of the food they found. According to them, they weren't homeless, but had chosen to live "off the grid," eating and using what had been cast off by others. By doing so, they had in effect disassociated themselves from capitalism and consumerism. They said they were living more ethically than me. I knew their rants were disingenuous and convoluted since they were still using gas and electricity to cook some of the scavenged food. And even though they disdained capitalist society, they were undoubtedly benefitting from it, utilizing the fruits of that waste. But I said nothing to them, my inertia was too great and I couldn't argue. Sometimes it was a lot easier to not eat, to just get out of their way.

***

For a very brief period of time, I seemed to lose my most precious asset—my mind. It happened when I considered robbing a bank in order to get myself out of the dreadful financial hole I found myself in. Things had derailed to the point where I was hardly employable, I knew that. The future looked incredibly bleak. I came to the conclusion that my life would be so much better if only I didn't have to worry about finances. And perhaps if I didn't have to concern myself with money, I'd be a different person. Happier. So the way I looked at it was that pulling off the heist was my last chance at respectability.

So I staked out the Royal Bank of Canada branch on Bloor Street. I had coffee at a donut shop right across the street. I found out that Saturday morning was when the bank carried the most cash; at exactly 11 a.m., Brinks security guards came for the cash that had built up during the entire week. So I had to get there before then. And I had no doubts that the money was safely ensconced within a safe, somewhere in the back of the building. But it was simple: I didn't see why it would be difficult putting a gun to a teller's head and telling them to hurry to the safe and enter the combination.

I considered the scenario long and hard. I wasn't a hardened criminal and certainly had never handled a gun before. Could I actually pull it off, robbing a bank? I concluded I could, but that the gun business was out … that I couldn't do. Not a real one, anyway. I would just use a fake gun. I found what I was looking for at a toy store on Yonge Street. It looked exactly like the real deal; it was even named after the Glock handgun … a *Glock Water Express Pistol*, able to squirt water at fast speeds. Quick reloading capacity. Long distances. I also bought an Uzi Sub-Machine Gun, another water gun.

"It has an open bolt," the salesclerk, a young girl with studded eyebrows and an oversized lip ring, said. She was chewing a big wad of gum and looked no older than eighteen. It was ridiculous, what could she possibly know about machine guns?

"It's a semi-automatic," she said, blowing a large bubble that popped loudly. "It was modelled after the true-to-life Israeli Uzi."

"I don't know anything about Israeli Uzis."

"Trust me."

"How much is it?"

"$49.95."

"That's expensive! Man, oh man."

"A real Uzi will cost you thousands and they'll have to do background checks."

So I bought it, just to get out of there. Money I didn't really have. Good thing there was Visa, I would settle with them in the distant future. The last thing I needed was a lecture on Uzis from a teenage girl.

"Would you like the extended warranty with that, sir?"

"They're plastic water guns," I said, shaking my head.

"I have to ask, sir. It's my job."

So I walked out with the replicate Glock and Uzi.

I was in way over my head but figured if I had gone this far, I might as well go all the way. So I went to a store specializing in Halloween costumes and bought a Mr. Penguin costume. Complete with a face mask and cape, I was a character straight out of a Batman movie.

"For my teenage son," I said to the clerk.

"Stuff left over from Halloween," the young man said. "We're getting rid of last year's costumes. That's why it's so cheap. Your son will love it."

At home, I put on the costume and held the Uzi across my chest. I stood in front of a full-length mirror and twirled round and round. Then I practised what I was going to say when I first entered the bank: "This is a bank robbery. Everyone down on the floor!" I knew exactly what I'd do next—bolt to the counter and confront the teller: "Hand over all your cash," I'd say quietly. "Don't you dare ring any alarms, if you know what's good for you. I don't want to hurt you but I will if necessary."

After a few days of pretend bank robbing, I packed up the guns and costume into a box and dropped the lot off at Goodwill, the second-hand store, overwhelmed with shame. "I can't believe I almost did this," I said to myself. "I'm going nuts."

And so that's what that one punch did for me. Threw me for a loop, into an alter-ego, a life I didn't want. But in hindsight, it could have been worse. I could have been thrown in jail. Besides, I made my point with the punch and it felt good to do so. Sometimes, you just had to stand up for yourself. I bore in mind what Niccolò Machiavelli once said about violence: "Upon this, one has to remark that men ought either to be well treated or crushed …"

THE STORY THIEF

I was an unemployed philosophy hack, turfed from the university's philosophy graduate program for punching out my academic mentor. It's a long story, and one I'd rather forget. But that one punch sent me into the murky world of the law where I was mandated to do community work, and attend group therapy sessions, where I met a woman by the name of Rachel Howard. I hardly knew her and, to the best of my recollection, she attended all of three or four meetings, barely saying a word throughout. Which to me seemed positively ridiculous: Why come to group therapy if you won't speak? I do recall that the facilitator prodded her but it was all for naught. She was as closed as a clam. What else? Ah yes, she was close to my own age, mid-thirties or so. And a cutter. That's what I remember most. During a break in a session, when we had both stepped outside the building for a smoke, I saw a series of ugly zig-zag scars on one of her arms. Her long sleeve shirt had somehow ridden up as she took a drag, revealing the misfortune. And as she swayed nervously from foot to foot, I also learned from her that she had a passion for books, her favourite writer being Virginia Woolf. It was during that brief encounter that I gave her my phone number, one book lover to an-other—but she never called.

* * *

One day I received a rather odd phone call from a woman named Ruth who claimed to be Rachel's land-lady, asking me to come by, saying that it was very im-portant. Very strange indeed and I had no idea what to expect. But since I was unemployed, with nothing much to do, I agreed.

The apartment building Rachel lived in was the kind you passed by quickly; the entrance was without a door and the smell of roach spray permeated the halls. The balconies stood like impenetrable fortresses around the lives of the inhabitants, protected with laundry lines of clothes, mattresses, and rusting bicycles. Three young toughs loitered in the lobby and eyed me suspiciously. "You got a smoke?" one said. His N.Y. Yankee hat was on backwards and his oversized black jeans hung halfway down his bum, revealing a pair of Looney Tunes cartoon underwear. I snuck a quick glance at Daffy Duck and handed over my entire pack of Du Mauriers.

"Here," I said. "I'm trying to quit anyway." I wasn't.

I recognized the name—*Whitmore*—on a wall plaque. The Whitmore Buildings were once part of a govern-ment-sponsored initiative to provide lower-income hous-ing for those in the arts. Rent was geared to income. But through mismanagement and cuts in provincial funding, the project fell apart and now housed impoverished im-migrants and those on the margins. The newspapers sometimes had stories of deaths in the buildings. Guns.

Knives. Gangs. Drugs were prevalent. So was prostitution. Most of the artists had moved out.

I met Ruth as planned. She had some sort of blue dishrag around her head, thin strands of mousey brown hair sticking out. Her eyes were beet-red, like she hadn't slept in days. She was terribly overweight. As a first impression, she was terribly, horribly, miserably, that's what she was and more, with legs peeking out from the far reaches of a dirty paisley smock like mottled balloons.

As we walked the length of the long, dark corridor with its peeling paint and frayed carpeting, I wondered how Rachel fit into the equation. Artist? Immigrant? Misfit? Surely not a moll or hooker. I only knew one thing: I felt I was marching to my execution—there was something terribly depressing and ominous about the place.

"The cops told me to look for a relative," Ruth said.

"I'm not a relative."

"Now you listen to me good—yours was the only phone number I could find in her address book. Somebody has to remove all the crap and it sure as hell ain't me."

When the door was opened, an indescribable smell wafted out, causing me to gag. Ruth held her nose. "She killed herself, maybe it was an accidental overdose. We found the tenant lying on the bed. There was an open bottle of sleeping pills next to her."

The tenant?

"What exactly do you want me to do here?" I said.

"Simple. I have to rent this place out again. I need you to clean it, take her stuff. Do whatever you want with it. *Capiche?*"

"What about the police?"

"Their investigation is over. It wasn't much of any-thing. They only asked a few questions: How long the tenant had lived in the apartment, did I know of any friends or relatives. That sort of thing. They didn't search the place, just went through her wallet. They looked at all the pills on the bed, saw how dirty the place was, and said 'we're done'. What did they call it? Oh yeah, *death by misadventure*."

"So how long *did* she live here?" I said. "And what about any friends?"

"A few years. Like I said to the cops, I keep to myself. I don't want no trouble. In this building, people come and go. What they do, who they know ... that's none of my business."

"Interesting."

"Maybe to you but not to me. It's a big hassle, that's all. Anyway, don't ask me nothing no more. Just get her things out."

"Excuse me. The woman died. Doesn't that mean anything ..."

"So?" the landlady said. "Is that *my* fault?"

For a second, I thought about telling Ruth to stuff it, she was a real piece of work. But I realized that, if I helped out, I might come to understand the mystery that was Rachel Howard. How, I wondered, had a bright woman in what should have been the prime of life sunk so low? Why had she lived in such decrepit circum-stances? The other thing that caused me to keep my mouth shut was that I realized the endeavour might do me good—I needed a distraction from the circum-stances of my own life.

Ruth took out a pack of Kleenex from her smock and gave it to me. "You'll need this for your nose."

I wandered through the apartment, a Kleenex covering my mouth and nose. The wallpaper was peeling in spots and the wall-to-wall carpeting was spotted with stains. Cigarette butts were everywhere. On the bathroom floor, I found a solitary razor blade. It was streaked with dried blood.

As utterly filthy and disgusting as the place presented, it was the smell that nearly caused me to double over. To say it was of decay would be too generous; it was as sharp and cutting as a garbage dump—a malodorous swamp of vomit, food, booze, cigarettes, and of things I couldn't name. It was nothing less than the sad refuse of life long since abandoned.

"Oh God, what is that?" I said, waving my hand in front of my nose.

"I don't know," Ruth said. "But whatever it is, I need it cleaned."

I pried open a jammed window with a butter knife I found in a kitchen drawer and stuck my head out for a breath.

There were stacks of newspapers and magazines piled everywhere, and unwashed plates and cutlery littered the sink where a family of roaches revelled amidst the food remains. A furry brown mouse scurried along a countertop, causing a fright in me.

"Are you going to pay me?"

Ruth rolled her eyes.

"I'll do what I can," I said, "but it might take a week or two to make this place look presentable. Maybe even longer."

"That's fine. I'm going to give you some boxes so you can put stuff away. After that, I don't want to see your face until this place is spic 'n' span. Got it?"

Stupid twit. "I'll need some gloves," I said. "There's no way I'm touching anything."

Ruth left me alone and I waited for her to return. Even Superman wouldn't have stood a chance against the smell. It was nothing less than decaying Kryptonite. I quickly held a second Kleenex up to my nose.

I was never happier to see someone than when Ruth walked back in. "Here, put these on."

I slipped the latex gloves on and tied a surgical mask around my face.

"Now I'm leaving," she said. "Here's the keys. I'm in 1A. I expect you to check in next Tuesday. One week."

I wandered through the apartment, surrounded by rot and feeling much like a zombie walking amidst the dead. I had hardly slept the night before, beset as I was with recurrent insomnia. I felt like passing out and briefly rested on one knee.

In a kitchen cabinet, I saw a myriad of pill bottles—Ativan, Xanax, Valium, Celexa, Zoloft—too many to get my head around. From my own bouts of depression, I recognized them as anti-depressants and anti-anxiety medications. Years earlier, during a particularly stressful period in my life, I had taken Celexa. I had to admit that it improved my mood considerably; I felt happy all the time. Almost euphoric. So much so that I couldn't sleep; I'd go for long walks in the middle of the night, venturing to parks to lay bird seed on the ground. And while my brain's happiness quotient greatly perked up, my other mental faculties did not. I walked around like the village idiot, a perpetual grin on my face ... and I couldn't think. After a few weeks on the drug, I wasn't able to muster up a single cogent thought; a thick fog shrouded the analytical side of my brain and the best I could do was repeat what others said. My school grades dropped precipitously and watching TV became a favourite pastime. Mind-numbing game shows mostly. After six months of this zombie-like behaviour, I packed the drug in.

As I looked through Rachel's pharmaceutical collection, what immediately stood out was that they had all been prescribed by different doctors. Multiple doctors, multiple medications ... it was a recipe for disaster.

In another cabinet, I found vitamin bottles. I recognized the most common ones—B and C, Calcium/Magnesium—but there were many others that I had no knowledge of: TG-100, Rhodiola, Ashwagandha. I conjectured that Rachel had probably tried to balance the pharmaceuticals with natural herbs and vitamins, that seemed the most logical explanation.

The apartment really was a pigsty. Things were flying about, grey, moth-like creatures that I smacked between my gloved hands. I slumped down into a tattered reclining chair in the living room and put my feet up. I reached for a small bottle on a coffee table and held it at eye-level. Chanel No. 5 perfume. Classic. 0.50 oz, the price tag clearly visible—$160. I lowered my mask and took a whiff. Mystical. Gossamers of exquisite flowers and herbs wafted to my nose, effectively blocking the horrid smell of my surroundings. Instinctively, my eyes closed momentarily as the scent descended upon me. The woman had taste, I couldn't deny it. I sat there motionless and stared at the bottle. If only she had said something to me. If only ...

I searched the drawers in the kitchen for a pack of cigarettes and found a carton of Gitanes Brunes. My lucky day. The Spanish gypsy woman on the black, blue and white cover was playing a tambourine. It wasn't lost on me that such an uplifting act was in sharp contrast to the bleakness of Rachel's apartment.

I sat back down in the chair and opened a slit in the mask for my lips. I lit a match and took a drag. The cigarette had a real bite. My entire body relaxed at once as I exhaled. I didn't stir, didn't blink. I simply sat and wondered why I was such an idiot for agreeing to clean the place. Chances were that I wouldn't uncover anything in Rachel's junk pile that would shed any insights into her. Even if there were, it struck me that I didn't really care. Hardly about anything and certainly not about some drug-crazed woman I didn't know. I had got myself into a stupid mess and now there was no backing out.

I stood up, walked to the sink and seared a distracted roach with the cigarette. It glowed like a red-hot ember and made a mad dash to safety behind the sink. I discarded the cigarette into a pot of murky water and left, the carton of Gitanes safely ensconced beneath my right armpit.

***

I returned the following day to Rachel's apartment, armed with two gym bags filled with cleaning utensils, disinfectant, and bug spray that I had picked up at Canadian Tire the night before. I liberally sprayed

Mandarin Orange and Sprightly Lemon from odour eliminator cans throughout and opened all the windows. I considered lowering my mask but decided against it; the air was still putrid. The perfume was where I had left it and I sprayed that too—undoubtedly Coco Chanel would not have approved of such blatant use but I needed every wonderful scent for my arsenal.

It was impossible to work with all the flying moths. They buzzed around my face like mad kamikaze pilots. The day before, I brought home a solitary one that I had squashed and compared its appearance with ones I found on the 'net. There was no question, these were pantry moths. I put up sticky moth paper on walls and shelves, on kitchen counters. In no time at all, the papers started filling up, the moths attracted to the phero-mones. It was utterly disgusting and all that was more than enough for one day.

* * *

I returned each day after that, always with a single daily project in mind. On Thursday and Friday, I worked on eradicating the vermin, roaches and mice. Saturday was set aside for the bathtub, which had a terrible black ring encrusted in the enamel. Sunday and Monday were for sanding the floors, and so on. I figured that if I set aside each day for just one task, that the whole affair might not seem so onerous. Dividing the tasks in such a man-ner seemed to work; once the smell abated somewhat and the mask was no longer necessary, I actually looked forward to visiting Rachel's apartment. It gave me some-thing to do.

My inclination though was to do a half-assed job. I hated anything to do with cleaning and rarely lifted a broom in my own apartment. But I surprised myself. I'm not exactly sure why. I surmised that it probably had to do with Newton's Second Law of Thermodynamics, the one that states that all things in a closed system tend toward maximum disorder, toward entropy, unless worked upon. And Rachel's apartment certainly embodied that chaos. So I would be the force that contravened the natural universal progression. I liked that, it made me feel somewhat powerful. A silly argument in favour of cleaning, I realized, but I always gravitated toward postulates.

I set wooden snap traps for the mice using bits of peanut butter as bait. I could hear the pop as the metallic spring came down hard on their necks; I didn't mind one little bit. I found in a local hardware store more humane mousetraps—box traps as they were known— complete with one-way doors that allowed the mice to enter but not escape. Unlike the snap-crackle-and-pop traps that I preferred, these could be used over and over again. But I wanted no part of them. It meant madly shaking boxes and taking the mice outside for release. That was a waste of my time: these were only vermin, after all.

Likewise, I set up motels of death for the roaches all throughout the apartment ... it was too easy. They crawled in and were stuck for all time. Just to be on the safe side, I also went through three cans of roach spray.

With the vast majority of the insects and such out of the way, working in the apartment became easier. The smell, although much improved, continued to linger and so each morning the first order of business was to give the place the once-over using a can of scent—Jasmine, Cinnamon, Green Apple. There were the more exotic ones too—Crisp Linen, Spring Waterfall, Ocean. And when I started washing the floors and countertops and threw away the stale food, the smell began dissipating even further. It improved dramatically when a week later I checked in with Ruth and she gave me permission to rip up the wall-to-wall carpeting. Little did I realize that when I did so, I would unearth even more creepy-crawlies … long and black, they were centipede-like things that were inordinately speedy. With their home exposed, they began darting to safety but in a mad scramble, I did my best to step on each and every one.

On the Tuesday, Ruth gave me cardboard boxes into which I could place all of Rachel's clothes. I had no use for the apparel of course and so my intention was to cart them over to Goodwill, the second-hand store. I still needed to concentrate on the apartment itself. Sure I had made some dents in getting it ready for Ruth to rent out, but there was no question that the place still required a lot of work. The bathtub, for instance, had that a black ring and try as I might, I just couldn't get rid of it. In fact, the more I scrubbed away at it, the blacker it became. Left with no options, I visited the same hardware store where I had purchased the mousetraps and ended up renting a palm sander. A palm sander, no less, something I had never even heard of before this Rachel caper unfolded! But once I got started restoring the apartment, I knew there was no point in taking shortcuts. So I used cheesecloth and a spray bottle to apply a chemical adhesive to the surface of the tub, and then painted on an acrylic polymer coating. In no time at all, and to my utter amazement, I had actually restored the tub to a white, pristine condition.

I did something similar with the wood flooring. I rented another piece of equipment of which I had no knowledge, a hand-held drum sander. Once I explained the situation, the hardware store manager was kind enough to throw in some used knee pads and safety glasses he had in the back for the job free of charge.

The flooring had enormous potential, even a lay person such as myself could see that. But it was all badly scuffed and nails were sticking out in spots. I swept the floor clean and pulled out the protruding nails. As I had been instructed, I then attached coarse sandpaper to the sander and began the operation. Once I got started, it was like maneuvering a Zamboni machine over a piece of ice ... the sander just slid along the grain. Once the first go-round was complete, I had to change the sandpaper to a finer grade and go over the entire flooring once again. Despite the ease with which the sander moved, it was nevertheless a daunting job. I worked in small squares and it took considerable time to finish. But finish I did, and then the floor was down to its natural wood. I might have then stained it but that in itself was a big job and as I had already spent a day and a half with the drum sander, I let it be.

Each day the place looked better and better. After every task I would sit in the recliner and reach for a smoke. Although I would never have imagined it, there was great satisfaction in completing a job. It made me feel somewhat competent, something that had been missing of late in my life. Sometimes though, a solitary moth would flitter by or I would spy a cockroach and that feeling would dissolve ...

* * *

I sifted through the stacks of newspapers to see if there was any reason or rhyme behind Rachel having kept them, but there was nothing. At least nothing I could determine—they were just yellowing pieces of newsprint hoarded by a mad collector. I bundled the entire collection and took them to the incinerator. I had no idea if you were allowed to throw paper into it but I didn't care … as long as I got rid of the lot.

I did find something of real interest: In the top drawer of a desk was Rachel's diary. Page after page of woe. There was great confusion about her health: she had been sick with some form of chronic fatigue that the doctors couldn't treat … or wouldn't treat, suggesting it was an imagined illness. There were money concerns and worries about her future. Loneliness. Boredom. Insomnia. Heart palpitations. A solitary quote from T.S. Eliot's *The Waste Land*—"I can connect / Nothing with nothing." Throughout there was no mention of any family or friends, no talk of trips or anything joyful. Bleakness.

On one page, I found mention of her excursions into back alleys to feed feral cats, many of whom she had given names … Oscar, Sonia, Luther … Early each morning she would slip out of the apartment to feed and water the homeless felines. That explained the many tins of cat food I found in the kitchen.

On the very last page, there was mention of stories she had written and that they afforded her a bit of joy. Something to hold onto.

* * *

It was all a lot of work, and took a lot of time. Fortunately, I had many days available in which to restore Rachel's apartment. I was ... well, temporarily unemployed. In between jobs, as they say. Mostly, I was always in between jobs. With a police record because of that one punch, it was hard to find jobs. My last job was selling lighting fixtures for a company in mid-town Toronto called The Lighting Emporium. It wasn't much, but did give me an opportunity to get a piece of writing published—"Replacing the Ballast in a Fluorescent Lighting Fixture." It appeared in *National Lighting & Fixtures Magazine*. I was a philosopher by trade or, let's say by ambition and inclination, but a wannabe fiction writer. So it wasn't exactly the kind of writing I wanted to be known for, but it was a start. In fact, it was my only piece of published material.

***

After two complete weeks in which my normally placid life was turned upside down, the onerous task of getting Rachel's apartment ready for the next tenant was done. The only thing left was to paint the place, but I was no painter. Someone else would have to finish the job. I took one last stroll around the once dismal apartment and realized that despite my hard work and good intentions, I had to get out of there. The apartment still radiated sadness, as if the walls had absorbed the worst of Rachel's broken life. I turned the keys over to Ruth.

"Find any treasures?" she said.

"Hardly. Mostly junk, as you said. Lots of books though."

"I know. I always told her it was a fire trap but she didn't listen. You have to be a little nutty to keep that many. What are they, trophies?"

"Definitely weird."

It really was weird. But not for the reason I portrayed to Ruth. I had spent two weeks sifting through another person's belongings, trying to put the pieces of a life together. In some ways I had done so, but in some other, more fundamental ways, I was no closer. The window into what had catapulted Rachel to the brink of darkness was closed. And probably would remain so for all time. And yet I had been a voyeur into her life. Yes, a voyeur, one who surreptitiously spies on another. It reminded me of a book I had once read—*Hell* by Henri Barbusse. Because the novel dealt with solipsism and existentialism, it had been part of the curriculum in a philosophy class. Even to this day, I can recall great chunks of it—the protagonist who resides in a Paris boarding house and who peeks through a hole in his bedroom wall to the room next door, where he observes the various lodgers who come and go. Not only does he witness birth and death, but so too adultery, incest, lesbianism, illness. A wide swath of humanity. And only after he feels that he had uncovered all of life's secrets does he decide to leave the room for good. But, as he is about to depart, he is overcome with blindness. Voyeurism, obsession, loneliness—at this time, the book spoke to me like no other.

***

In the bottom drawer of Rachel's dresser was the very last thing I would take from the apartment. Hidden under socks and underwear was a box; I tucked it tightly under my right arm and exited the apartment.

The sides of the box had been sealed with scotch tape and I conjectured that it might contain something worthwhile ... otherwise, why seal it? I was brimming with excitement all the way home and barely stopped myself from slipping a peek in the subway. But I resisted, thinking some nosy person in an adjoining seat might see the treasure trove as well. But when I got home and ripped the box open, I was startled to see that it only contained papers.

I sifted through the find. These were Rachel's written works, what she had referred to in her diary. There must have been thirty or so short stories along with a half-completed novel.

Rachel had been a basket case and I suspected that her work could only be garbage. But there might have been something in it that would shed further light on her plight, so I decided that I would read at least a few pages, maybe an entire forgettable story. But a most curious thing happened as I read—I continued. I read not one but many stories. They were so intriguing, so well-written, that after I began reading them, I was astounded.

Now I understood why Rachel had mentioned in her diary that writing had brought a measure of happiness—the woman had talent; she was very, very good. One story concerned an aspiring writer who takes a most unusual job, posing as a patient with a debilitating illness. In another, a woman who can't find a job with her liberal arts degree decides to rob banks. There was a riveting piece that dealt with a man giving up his conventional life in Toronto to go live a more bohemian lifestyle in Paris. The winners kept on coming. I particularly liked the one about an anarchist who finds peace after nursing a sick animal to health, and yet another that profiled a woman who pines for the poet she used to be.

There were small edits on each page, changes in red ink. A word, a sentence, nothing major. And each story had her name in a header at the top. Rachel's work. There was no indication that she had ever tried to get any of it published. She probably wrote for catharsis, something she could hold on to as the rest of her life went astray. Besides, there was probably one very good reason she never submitted anywhere. Because the risk in doing so is rejection. And from what I now understood of Rachel, that would have been intolerable for her.

The stories were all fairly short, under five thousand words for the most part. As might be expected, many of them dealt with alienation, people who were outsiders. I concluded that the central theme that permeated throughout was the idea of *loss*. Loss of a spouse, of integrity and ideals, loss of innocence and soul. Wide-ranging, they ran the gamut of the subject. They also focused on strange decisions the protagonists took to deal with those losses. The job applicant who was turned down for a position in a law firm decides to steal a Hermès scarf from that firm's cloak room. And the woman who could not find a job with her newly minted liberal arts degree makes an unusual career move by becoming a bank robber. Wonderful flights of fancy all, with unexpected twists.

What a shame, such a waste. If only Rachel had had the nerve to send her work out, she might have had some success. No, she *would* have had success, the material was that good. I felt certain of it. And success was exactly what her miserable life needed.

I thought long and hard about what to do with the collection. I considered just tossing it but that seemed foolish. I also contemplated self-publishing the stories into a booklet: *Rachel Howard: The Collected Short Stories*. I did turn over the notion that I might approach publishers with her story, that she was a depressed druggie who ultimately killed herself. But one with realms of talent. It might have been appealing to some publisher.

But I didn't do any of those things. I simply couldn't go through with them. Even vanity publishing was not inexpensive and as it were, I had barely enough money to live on. Moreover, dead was dead and so who really cared if the stories were published under Rachel's name or not? She had no friends, no relatives that would take great comfort from the publication of her gems. I had to admit it, not even I cared. Not really. Why would I? She was a virtual stranger. Besides, no one can deny that to the living go the spoils.

After a week of fooling around, doing some of my own edits, I was ready with the short stories. I picked a few of the top literary magazines in the country as my targets and packaged off a single story to each. In the cover letter, I said that the story had not been previously published and that I hoped it was suitable for the magazine. I made no mention of the fact that I hadn't written it. I still had vague thoughts that I would rectify that omission should the need arise. I suspected however, that that would never become necessary; getting published was no small feat and as good as the story was, if my own work had been turned down, there was no reason to believe Rachel's would fare any better. It was true. Years ago, I submitted a short story to a magazine, *The New Yorker* no less, and it was turned down. It was heartbreaking and I never submitted another story to any place again.

***

Much to my surprise, a story entitled "Taking what is yours" was accepted. Accepted! Buoyed by that success, I sent out more stories and in relatively short order, six short stories were published in literary magazines and anthologies. Yet another story rose to even greater heights, placing second in the prestigious *Toronto Star* short story contest. It netted me $2,000, a princely sum in the literary world. A photo of me accompanied the piece, which was called "The Boy who doesn't Talk." Of all of my stories, it was perhaps the quirkiest, about a young boy who believes he is not from the earth. In order to stay remote from humans, he communicates solely by singing, never talking. He learns the words to over six-hundred songs and the doctors devise a new medical label for him—Lyric Savant. Essentially it meant someone who can't speak in normal language but is so gifted and disordered that he can learn hundreds upon hundreds of songs by rote. The protagonist is exactly like that—he finds styles of music for every occasion: rap and hip-hop provide all the fuel for his anger, country music the words for when he is hurting, folk music for revealing his maudlin side, pop and easy-listening for virtually everything else. And while he waits each night in the backyard for the mothership to take him back to his planet, the reader comes to understand the genesis of his disorder—his father has abused his mother and him for years.

As my writing started soaring to new heights, I began to make significant improvements with other matters. There seemed to be a corollary of sorts: As A (my writing) improved, then B (the rest of my life) followed suit. I suppose it all had to do with the fact that I felt better about myself. I was a philosopher, sure, but now I was a published writer. It was all as if I didn't have a say in the matter, success after success rolled on. Under constant badgering from employment counselors at EI, I even landed a job selling frozen meats from the back of a van. I wasn't particularly suited for most jobs—which is why I never lasted very long at any—but this one allowed me to make my own hours and offered the incentive of three weeks paid vacation, a rarity in the world of sales. In addition, I was given a list of steady customers residing in Forest Hill, Toronto's hoity-toity enclave of the rich. For some reason, the people there tolerated my aloofness. They weren't much different themselves, simply buying the meats and avoiding chit-chat. As jobs go, it was a good one.

I also did something that I would have previously abhorred—I took out a profile on Facebook. I had always considered social networking sites the domain of the very narcissistic; imagine, with the click of a keystroke, you could become "friends" with people you had never met nor spoken to. Still, despite my distaste for it, I slowly came to the realization that artists should probably have an online presence. The entire world was connected digitally, there was no denying. So I sent out "friend requests" and quickly amassed two-hundred-

and-seventy-five cyber-friends, all of whom were in one way or another connected to the Canadian literary scene. What was equally interesting was that I started to receive some friend requests of my own; it was becoming abundantly clear that people knew who I was. Yes, there could be no doubt, I was morphing into someone of note in this world, an *Ubermensch*. The philosopher Nietzsche's Superman! A man of influence, a man of status, that people admired and looked up to. It was all coming together now.

***

One rainy and cold day, just about ten months or so after I had my first short story published, I received a rather unusual and disturbing phone call.

"Is that Karl Pringle?"

"You've got him."

"This is Jeff Charles."

"Sorry but the name doesn't ring a bell."

"Look, I'm going to get right to the point. I just wanted to tell you that I read 'The Boy who doesn't Talk' in the *Toronto Star*. It's a great story."

"Thank you. I try my best and sometimes luck runs my way."

"That's my story!" Jeff shouted.

"What?! I don't know what you mean."

"Sure you don't. Well let me refresh your memory. That story appeared in a British magazine called *Bonfire* about three years ago. I guess you figured that you could get away with it because it's in a British magazine that's now defunct."

I was trembling and couldn't speak.

"Ok, well. I'm not sure exactly how to handle this. Maybe a lawyer would know better. But one thing I will do right off the bat is contact the *Toronto Star*. I'll tell the organizers of the contest they were duped. Shame, Karl. Shame."

The phone went dead.

I ran my hand back and forth through my hair. Every fibre in my body felt taut, on edge. I had no reason to disbelieve Jeff; why would he lie? I would have to check it out for myself. I went online and found *Bonfire Magazine*. And there it was in a back copy, "The Boy who doesn't Talk." My hands turned clammy and I felt light-headed. I turned to the story, the author was clearly stated as Jeff Charles.

How could I be so stupid? How could I think that a severely depressed woman juggling copious amounts of pharmaceuticals would write brilliant prose? I now realized that all Rachel had done was copy the story word-for-word from *Bonfire* onto her computer, put her name down as the author, made a few small edits (presumably to fool herself that she was the true author) and printed it out. The whole act had undoubtedly served to pacify her angst. And that was why she had never submitted the story to literary magazines or anywhere else. As loopy as she was, she knew better.

My mind raced. What about the other stories? I Googled the names of many of the stories in Rachel's collection. I found them all, in various magazines.

* * *

Jeff Charles was as good as his word. He advised the *Toronto Star* and very quickly I received a registered letter from them. It talked about how they had done some due diligence with regard to their short story contest and discovered that my story "The Boy who doesn't Talk" had been previously published. The third-place winner would be moved into my second place slot and the fourth-place finisher, who had obviously been out of the awards, would slide to third place. There would be a retraction of my story in an upcoming edition of the newspaper. The kicker however, was that I was to immediately pay back the $2,000 they had given me. There was a due date for the return of the money. Legal action would be instituted if I failed to do so. It was not what one might call a friendly letter. Hardly, it was rather pointed.

***

After I had destroyed the last of Rachel's "writings," I spent most days lounging in bed, smoking joints and staring at the television. The remote zoomed through the channels, my unseeing eyes riveted to the screen.

I stopped showing up at work and eventually lost my job selling meats. Not going out meant there was no reason to wash—I could almost smell the fermentation of my own skin but the inertia was more powerful.

One thing I managed to do was go on Facebook. I hadn't been on for quite a while, not since I started accumulating friends on the site because of my literary success. Now I saw the real carnage from my theft. The retraction that appeared in the *Toronto Star* had been posted directly onto my home page. The headline screamed out: "Toronto Writer Plagiarizes Story." There were plenty of comments from those cyber friends of mine and sufficed to say, not one was supportive. They slandered me, calling me a slimeball, a disgrace to the human race, a piece of gunk that sticks to the bottom of your shoes. It went on and on. Some suggested that I be burned in a cauldron of bubbling oil, or flogged. One person wrote that I should do the right thing and hang myself. I had no idea humanity could stoop that low.

I began to take stock of my life and it wasn't good. Every door that had once been open for me began closing. And I was the author of my own misfortune. All because I thought I was an alchemist who could turn lead into gold. An alchemist, imagine. Maybe that was the lesson in all this, that I should surrender and understand what I was ... and what I wasn't. I was no alchemist from medieval Europe. I didn't have an alchemist's flask. I didn't even have the Philosopher's Stone, the legendary unknown substance that could turn base metals into precious ones. Rather, I was a philosopher of some note and I would have to accept that.

THE HOVEL

I lived in a small one-bedroom above a butcher shop in Kensington Market. I loved living in the Market, surrounded by vintage clothing stores, fragrant cheese shops, an African hand-drum store, and even the fish market where crabs crawled over each other in aquarium tanks. It was a cornucopia of diverse humanity, where this century's newly ordained hippies mingled with Italian grocers and Portuguese sausage makers, and where everyone, no matter how off-beat, fit in perfectly. Even the shabby man who wore a long white robe and proclaimed to be Jesus was well tolerated. And the apartment served my needs well. It was cheap and close to the university, functional. Other than that, not many more attributes could be said of it. The paint was peeling, the floors were sticky, and occasionally, during the cold days of winter, it would lose all heat for a few hours, causing me to wear layers of clothing, draped over with blankets. Roaches were prevalent and oftentimes the smells from the butcher shop below wafted through my window, causing me to gag. Bloody animal innards. For that, there was a simple solution, I discovered—keep the window closed year-round. And flower the apartment with the aroma of weed, which I did quite often. Basically, I lived in a hovel. A squalid garbage dump.

Down the hall lived the tenant in an adjacent apartment. An eighty-something-year-old woman (so I surmised), crippled with rheumatoid arthritis and with a touch of dementia, was my neighbour. If the woman could've cooked like my late mother, it might have been alright. Instead, because she seemed to constantly keep her door open, when I went into the hallway I had to endure the smells—open cans of mackerel and tuna mixed with chopped onions and some monstrosity called blood pudding, a sausage made with dried pig's blood and oatmeal as a filler. The slaughtered remains of the goats and cows from the butcher shop downstairs sometimes seemed like exquisite perfume in comparison. If all that weren't enough, my neighbour, who went by the unlikely name of Brenda Bumblegate, would try and regale me not only with her cooking exploits but also with tales of her life in show biz, where she said she often worked as a character actor. Apparently, she starred alongside Buster Keaton, which I highly doubted. With Brenda's appetite for deep-red lipstick, copious amounts of mascara and face powder, a beehive hairdo, it was like living down the hall from a half-baked Bette Davis.

"I did work with Buster, you know, Karl," she would say. "He had a thing for me, but I rejected him all the time. He had terrible bunions and I couldn't stand to look at them. Bony bumps, my God. I suppose I could have asked him to keep his shoes on all the time but who keeps their shoes on when they're making love? Who, Karl, who?"

"Nobody I know."

"Exactly. So don't think I'm a bad person. You don't think I'm a bad person, do you, Karl?"

"No, Brenda, I don't."

"I'm pretty delightful, don't you think?"

"I'm not sure I would go that far."

"What do you mean by that?"

"Nothing. Nothing. You're pretty delightful."

So it was to this glorious apartment that I retreated every night and it was there that I was able to indulge in my favourite pastime—playing the online game *Dark Age of Camelot*. I don't recall the exact moment when I started *Camelot*, only that I have been immersed in the wonderful online fantasy gaming world for many, many years. Certainly all throughout my undergraduate years. I do know that when I read Amazon's summation of the game as being perfect for those who "do not play well with others," I was hooked. Aristotle said that "excellence is an art won by training and habituation." Of course! I had to excel and could only do so by playing constantly.

I suppose much of my interest in *Camelot* rests in the fact that the game resides in fantasy. I have always needed a break from the *real* world. But it's more than just that: the game speaks to me in ways people cannot. Throughout my life I have run into forgers and shiftless people, rogues, but not so in *Camelot*. Yes, yes, I know King Arthur is dead and so the three realms he presided over rest in a precarious state of peace. For the uninitiated, the realms are known as Albion, Hibernia, and Midgard. Following the good king's death, they waged war against each other, vying for control of keeps and towers, relics, and the entrance to Darkness Falls. Accumulation of points is of paramount importance. Players are awarded Realm Points for each enemy realm player they kill.

I've spent many days and nights playing. There have been so many wonderful memories. *Camelot* is pure magic, distinct from any other game. It blows all others out of the water as far as I'm concerned. I realize that what I've said about the game might seem trivial to some, but I don't care. Let me simplify it: I feel that my actions in *Camelot* can have a real tangible result, that's what I'm saying. In this other-world, I can reclaim power and work toward the advancement of mankind. I can advance a new generation of beings, bigger, stronger, and more astute. And I can be the leader; I can save the wretched world and turn into Nietzsche's *Ubermensch*. A superman. A man with his own set of morals and ethics who dominates and affects those of others. A man capable of amazing achievements. A leader of men. A man who alters history. I once read a line by Virgil, the great Roman poet: *Audaces fortuna iuvat*. He was right, fortune does favour the bold. It was also slowly starting to crystallize for me that maybe this was the start of my becoming Nietzsche's Superman, the *Ubermensch*. *Camelot* and Superman, a perfect union.

Ah, Nietzsche, the 19th century German philosopher that I studied in university. It seems to me that he had it right. That mankind has been mired in morals imposed by others, by institutions, by the church, synagogue, whatever. It led to an unthinking group of automatons, willing to be led to slaughter. Just like the animals that were meekly rounded up and butchered, ended up hanging in the windows of the shop below my apartment. I wasn't like that; I had my own set of morals, not imposed on me by others. I was too aware to be rounded up. I didn't know exactly how I could be the man that

Nietzsche talked about. But as a baby step, I could start in *Camelot*. Take it from there.

***

One evening, after having spent the entire day sitting under a tree reading a book and contemplating a blade of grass, even sliding it in my mouth to taste, I returned home to see that the narrow flight of stairs leading up to my apartment was occupied. Two young men were balancing a massive leather sofa, trying desperately not to be crushed.

"Hold your end up more," the guy at the very top said.

I was concerned that the guy at the bottom end was going to tumble backward into me. He seemed to be losing his grip. As it was, there was no getting to my place. I moved a few steps back and waited.

It was like watching a Laurel and Hardy movie. The two movers kept on giving each other instructions that turned out badly. Both wanted to be in charge of the operation and each step forward was a misstep; the sofa wouldn't fit around the corner so they tried lifting the sofa on its end ... then it was too high for the ceiling.

"Maybe we should just cut it in half," one said.

"Yah, you wouldn't say that if it was your sofa," his friend said.

After some twenty minutes or so in which the movers fumbled and bumbled their way up the stairs, taking a chunk of the plaster from the wall with them, the deed was done. They sat down exhausted onto the sofa, huffing mightily and holding their heads.

"Fuck, I can't believe we made it."

"If you had only listened to me, we would have made it much quicker."

That started a whole new row where name-calling became the order of the day. I couldn't tell the two apart; they were slope-shouldered lanky youths in their late teens or early twenties and with identical shaggy-dog haircuts that covered their eyes. They blew gusts of air upward to lift the hair, only to have the strands fall back. The only difference that I could see was that one was wearing a Che Guevara T-shirt and the other an overly large checked lumberjack shirt.

"Is this for Bumblegate?" I said.

"Who's Bumblegate?" the Che Guevara guy said, eyeing me suspiciously. "And who are you?"

"I live just down the hall."

"Uh, huh."

"Mind if I sit down?"

"Take a load off, dude," Che said.

I sat between the two. "I see you're wearing a Che T-shirt," I said. "Do you know who he was?"

"Dude, are you my like history teacher or some-thing? Of course I do."

"So?"

Che sat up straight. "He was like the leader of a revo-lution. *Re-vo-lu-tion* as they say in Cuba," he said, put-ting a heavy accent on the last syllable. "He was backing the Sandinistas because they were oppressed."

Lumberjack guy chimed in. "Like man, you are so out of it. He was backing the *Federales*, not the Sandinistas, you jackass."

Another round of vicious name calling began, punc-tuated by bursts of fists that bounced off each other's shoulders. Seeing as how I was caught directly in the line of fire, I interjected: "Hey, hey, calm down!" I nudged them back to their respective corners of the sofa.

No question, I was sitting in the middle of two clowns. But who were they anyway? I didn't really care much, but I was curious. Still, I tried to keep the conversation going.

"You guys must be in school, I take it?"

"Yeah," lumberjack guy said, exhaling deeply and feigning another lunge at his nemesis.

"What're you studying?"

"The same thing," he said.

"And what's that?"

"Video gaming. We're gonna be designers."

"Centennial College, that's where we go," Che said, now much calmed down.

I thought it would be a good idea to advise them of my interest in *Camelot*. It wasn't.

"*Camelot*?" Che said, smirking. "That is like so fuckin' old. Dude, nobody plays that anymore."

"I have to agree with my lame brother here," lumberjack guy said. "That technology is like hundreds of years old. It is so crippled."

I wasn't sure what he meant by that but understood that it wasn't good. Suddenly Che took out a joint and pointed it at me. "Want to join?"

"Sure."

We passed the fag around and as I inhaled deeply, a new sense of calm washed over me.

"So what do you do?" Che asked, his head lolling back.

"Nothing much. But I have this idea I'd like to write books."

"Like on paper?"

"Yes, like on paper."

"Dude, that is so passé," lumberjack guy said. "Nobody reads books anymore. Soon it'll go like the way of Latin."

"You mean Pig Latin?" I said.

"Isn't that what I just said? Do you ever hear anyone speak it anymore?"

In a twisted way, he had a point.

"The problem with books," Che said, sounding very professorial, "is that after you read the first page, there's like another three hundred pages of the same after that."

"Yeah, he's right," lumberjack guy said. "Nobody wants to read that much. Nobody should *have to* read that much. If you can't make your point in one-hundred-dred-and-forty characters, like on Twitter, then you should shut up."

Che clapped his hands. "Yep, there's no question," he exclaimed excitedly. "You see, because man, even if you somehow feel the need to go over that limit, you can stop! Put in emots."

"I don't know what that is."

The brothers looked at each other and sniggered.

"Like from the 17th century, dude," lumberjack guy said to his brother.

"I know. Such a wanker." Che pulled on his T-shirt. "Even this guy would know. And he was born way long ago, before you."

"But he's dead."

"Yah but when he was alive, I bet you he would know."

"So tell me."

"Emots are graphics to express how you feel. You ever see those happy faces on computers?"

I nodded.

"That's an emot."

"Oh, you mean *emoticons*," I said.

"That's exactly what I said," Che said, laughing in derision. "What a wanker."

Lumberjack guy took over. "Man, you don't even need words like in your text. You can say everything you want to say just by putting in those emots. Everyone will know what you're getting at."

I stood up. "It's been a blast fellas, but I have to go." I hesitated for a moment. "My name's Karl, by the way. And oh yeah, before I forget, what about this couch? Are you delivering it for Bumblegate again?"

The guys looked at each other once again and shook their heads. "Like we said, we don't know who that is," Che said.

"The old lady who lives in that apartment," I said, pointing. "Brenda Bumblegate."

"Oh her," Che said. "She died a few weeks ago. Me and my brother here are moving stuff in, kind of gradually. We've already been in three weeks now."

I was stunned. Bumblegate had died? When? And why hadn't anyone notified me? I asked the boys if they knew.

"The landlord said he knocked on your door many times," lumberjack guy said, "but that you never answered."

"You should always answer your door, even if you're not around," Che said. "Then people will know if you're home or not."

I walked into my apartment and crashed onto the bed, arms and legs spread eagle. It made sense now that

I thought of it. I had spent a lot of time of late wandering the city, and hadn't been in the apartment all that much. Still, the death struck me hard. It's not that I cared in the least for the woman; she was a miscreant. It's just that when you live in an acrobat tent like Kensington Market, or more specifically, my apartment building, you get used to the clowns and freaks that populate the tent. All the circus performers. They become like family. You always expect that they'll be there, no matter what. That things will remain the same. And unfortunately, they never do.

I went online and found an obit:

Brenda Patricia Bumblegate

In Loving Memory
It is with deep sadness we say goodbye to Brenda Patricia Bumblegate, affectionately known to her friends and family as 'Bumble Bee.' To say that Brenda lived life to the fullest would be an understatement. She embraced life and infected all those who had the good fortune to know her with that same spirit. An avid sailor, world traveller, actor, musician, she played the harmonica and keyboards in her jazz trio with the same aplomb that saw her scale Everest to base camp.

In a loving partnership of 30 years with her husband Solly, who passed away in 2015, Brenda thrived in the company of her children and grandchildren, friends and colleagues. She was cherished by those who knew her: her husband

Solly, daughter Caroline, son Charles, sisters Irene Baltsch of Ottawa and Heidi Travers of Norfolk, Virginia, granddaughters Kathy and Gwendolyn.

Of all her passions, Brenda perhaps loved performing most of all. She acted on stage in both Toronto and N.Y. and appeared in numerous films as a character actor alongside luminaries like Joan Crawford, William Holden, Maureen O'Hara, Robert Mitchum, Buster Keaton, and many others.

THE BOOK SALE

nce, when I was very short on money, I decided to hold a book sale. I thought it was a brilliant idea and was missing only one thing—books. So I biked all around the city on my handy ten-speed and frequented as many of those little lending libraries that I could. The ones perched on wood stakes in front of people's lawns where you were to *take a book, donate a book*. It took me weeks to accumulate a big cache of very decent books, mostly literature. Serious books. Dickens, Coetzee, James, Woolf, D.H. Lawrence, Borges, Richler, Auster, Doyle, Orwell, Byatt ... a large library of important writers. With my interest in existential writers, I recognized Camus and Sartre and Bukowski. I opened Sartre's *No Exit* and read his most famous of lines: "Hell is other people." Clever guy. It was amazing that I could find all these great books that people willingly gave away. For a brief moment, I contemplated that perhaps I should keep them all, given that I loved reading. They would provide me with comfort, constant companions during times of strife, which was just about all the time. But the lure of making a bit of extra cash was too great.

Now that I'd solved the problem of accumulating books to sell, I realized I had a second, equally pressing problem—my apartment was a pigsty. I would have to fix it up a bit. More than a little bit. It was terribly unappealing, drab and ugly. It also smelled from all the weed I smoked almost daily. I had crappy furniture picked up from garage sales and exactly four dishes, all of which were cracked.

So I set out to make the apartment look presentable. I hired two students from the university to paint the place a cerulean blue and wash the stickiness off the floors. They came cheap so I didn't mind—I paid them a bit and gave them some joints to call it even. I bought a set of dishes from a bargain-basement department store, along with drinking glasses, coffee cups, and a few plates. I called an ad on Craigslist and struck a deal for a brown faux-leather sofa and two corduroy tub chairs. They were a bit worn, but considerably better than the furniture I had. The couple who sold them even drove the goods over in their SUV. At Goodwill, I lucked upon an embroidered bedspread, a crystal vase into which I plunked some dried flowers, and a sturdy wooden coffee table. I also biked around to garage sales. At one, I purchased three framed van Gogh posters and four area rugs. And at another, four black bookcases made of pressboard that I carried home one at a time, each firmly perched on my shoulder. As a final touch, I bought a couple of plants.

All this cost me a bit of money—not much, but I figured I would make it back and more from the sale. As I looked around the apartment, I was surprised how much I had done in such a short period of time. And how much better the place looked. Decent enough to have people over for a sale. As a final touch, I sprayed with air freshener to displace the skanky smell of dope. That was it. A job well-done.

I didn't have enough bookcases to house all the books but there was nothing much I could do about that—I just piled them onto the kitchen table, the coffee table, kitchen counters, window sills, stored many in plastic milk crates, baskets ... everywhere. There wasn't a cranny left in the apartment where a book had not taken up residence. It all resembled the work of a mad hoarder.

I priced all the books with small sticky notes and then set out to place flyers advertising the event. I ventured to the English Department of the University of Toronto, where I found a suitable bulletin board. After, I made my way to a number of coffee shops along Bloor Street—Second Cup, Starbucks, Paulo's Espresso Bar—where I posted the flyers. Then to the very bohemian Kensington Market where I lived, which is always ripe for artsy events such as the one I was promoting. The Moonbeam Café was my first stop, followed by the Baldwin Café. I even stood on the corner of Baldwin Street and Kensington Avenue, handing out the flyers.

"Please come," I said. "It's for a good cause."

While some people were congenial and asked questions about the sale, even going so far as saying they would show up, others were outright rude.

"What you selling, boy, I have no interest," one man said, giving me a dismissive wave with his hand. He had a big Afro and wore gold chains around his neck. "Don't give me no shit papers." He was walking alongside his bike and steered it dangerously toward me, veering off at the last possible second.

I called CIUT, the university's radio station, and pleaded with them to find some air time to promote the sale. I told them that all proceeds would go to SickKids Hospital. I wasn't exactly sure that that was the case; I hadn't worked out all the details. But I thought saying as much would elevate the occasion to a charitable event and bring in more people.

At 9 a.m. on the day of the sale, knowing full well that I would have to interact with a bunch of strangers, I took an Ativan just to chill out. I made two pots of coffee and set out a few boxes of chocolate chip and Oreo cookies onto the table. I took one last look around the apartment and at 9:30 opened the door, where a line of customers had already formed.

"Come in, come in," I said. "I'm so glad you're all here."

Glad you're all here? It didn't matter, I was just trying to be jocular, convivial. It was not lost on me that those were words not normally found in my vocabulary.

I was approached by a particularly pretty thing with multicoloured hair. Red and purple and blue. She was perhaps twenty-five or so and wearing UGG sheepskin boots, ones I knew all the fashionistas of the world wore and which I detested.

"Any Harold Robbins here?" she said.

"You've got the wrong sale, honey."

"How about Sidney Sheldon?"

I shook my head.

"Nora Roberts?"

I walked over to a bookshelf and plunked out D.H. Lawrence's *Lady Chatterley's Lover*.

"This is for you," I said. "I think you'll like it. It's full of sex and intrigue."

"Rad, how much?"

"For you, it's free. Have an Oreo."

People sat in chairs, on the sofa, on the floor, and read. Dawdled and munched on cookies. I didn't mind. The Ativan had set in and my mood was light, almost ephemeral. Even when I was approached by those who wanted to haggle over the prices, I was not particularly bothered. I merely explained that the listed amounts were cheap enough and that the proceeds were meant to help children in need. Cancer patients. Everyone quickly relented.

It was mostly the usual suspects who attended. Owners of second-hand book shops, students, a few professors wearing worn tweed jackets. "You've got good taste," I was told numerous times. To which I simply replied: "Thank you."

I recognized the owner of an antiquarian book shop —John Fraser. Our paths had crossed on many an occasion when I purchased philosophy books at the store. Sometimes we met at university lectures that were open to the public. We also knew some of the same people.

I felt uncomfortable seeing John, given that I was no longer in school and would have preferred to avoid him. But needless to say, the apartment was too small and so we swaggered slowly toward each other like gunslingers meeting at high noon. I extended a friendly hand. "John Fraser," I said. "It's been a long time."

"How are you, Karl? I didn't know you had such a collection. Philosophy, yes. But literature?"

The jig was up; I revealed a version of the truth. "Selling these books for a friend. She moved to Amsterdam and won't be coming back. She wanted all the proceeds to go to the hospital. She's got a heart of gold."

"Would I know her?"

"I don't think so. Her name is Joan Roland. Went to Concordia and then York. Not U of T. She had an interest mostly in Victorian literature. Dickens, Brontë, Jane Austen."

"Austen was really pre-Victorian."

"That's true. That's true. Anyway, I think you get the idea. Great collection of books, don't you think?"

"I'm quite interested in a couple of first editions here. Atwood, Isherwood, and Orwell." John waved the books in front of me. "How much?"

"I hadn't priced those, John, simply because they were first editions. What do you think is fair?"

I accepted John's first offer, telling him that we were old friends. Really, I just wanted him out before he started delving into my now non-existent studies at the university. Fortunately, it worked. John took the books and walked out the door. "Drop by the shop," he said as parting words. "I've got some rare David Hume and Plato books you might be interested in."

The sale went on all day. By four o'clock I was bushed. Not only had I sold almost the entire library but I had also chatted with numerous people. I even exchanged phone numbers with a few. At five o'clock, I ushered the last of the people out the door and slumped into the reclining chair. That was it, the deed done. I counted the loot—$964. I grabbed a coffee and a handful of chocolate chip cookies, which I downed with great satisfaction. It truly had been an amazing day.

***

I considered what to do with the money and decided upon a new computer and printer. No charitable donations!

There would probably be a few bucks left over to purchase some weed. I realized very good computer equipment would cost me more money than what I had. So I sourced the Market for some black market goods and lucked out. A man named Carlos was well-known for selling top-notch computers from his truck. You only had to have the right contacts to know that.

In no time at all, I met Carlos in an alleyway where he slid open the doors of his truck to reveal a treasure trove of high-end computers.

"What you like, my friend?"

He called me "my friend." I liked that.

I settled on a Canon printer and an Acer desktop. So much better than the computer equipment I had at home. Carlos even helped me bring it upstairs and configure things. I paid him and gave him two joints.

* * *

A week after the purchase, there was a knock on the door. Two men introduced themselves and flashed badges. Detectives. They were big in stature, each over two hundred pounds by my estimate, and I felt somewhat puny next to them, what with my dripping-wet one-hundred-and-sixty pounds.

"This won't take long," one of the cops said. He had a great handlebar moustache that looked as if you could hang two kettle handles from, one at either end of the upsweep.

"Can I see your badges again?" I asked flippantly. I wouldn't take shit from them, no fuckin' way. As big as they were, I knew my rights.

Only the handlebar guy obliged. The other, a stout man with a bull neck, simply looked pissed.

Detective Graziano Quilico.

"My father was a big boxing fan," the detective said, putting his badge away. His buzz-cut hairstyle was a throwback to another era.

"He loved a boxer by the name of Graziano. That's how I got my name. Everyone calls me Gracie but it's short for Graziano."

I gazed attentively at Gracie. What was with the small talk? If he wanted to arrest me, he should have just got on with it. I hadn't done anything wrong anyway.

"So what can I do for you?" I asked Gracie. I didn't look at the other cop.

"How long have you lived here?" he said.

"A few years."

"Do you know someone called Edgar Giardano?"

"Nope. Never heard of him."

"He goes by the street name of 'Carlos'," Gracie said.

"Actually . . ."

"What did you buy from him?"

Oh shit. Maybe I could throw myself upon the mercy of the courts and get a reduced sentence. Maybe plead insanity.

"He sells stolen goods," Gracie said. "We've been after him for months now."

I sheepishly pointed to the computer and printer sitting on the kitchen table.

"You realize knowingly buying stolen goods is a criminal offence."

"I didn't know they were stolen," I said, squeaking. "I swear."

"Well, we have to take them back to the station as evidence. Someone will be here in a few minutes." Gracie spoke into his phone and provided my address to the person at the other end.

I hung my head and when two other officers entered the apartment and carried the computer equipment off, I took an Ativan and crashed onto my bed. Damn, I should have known better. What a dufus I was. If Carlos was a creature of back alleys, it meant he couldn't be trusted. In all the time I lived in the Market, I never saw a single slimy rat on the streets. But I sure as hell knew they slunk around in the filth of the desolate alleys, at the rear of stores, out of sight.

But Gracie, what a piece of work he was! Who did he think he was taking away my hard-earned goods? With my eyes closed, I envisioned a boxing match in a ring between us. This was going to be Ernest Hemingway vs. Morley Callaghan all over again. Having had a strong interest in the many artists and writers who lived in 1920s and 30s Paris, I once read about their legendary fight. Hemingway was the much larger of the two men, an avid outdoorsman, a hunter and fisherman. But Callaghan was the more experienced boxer, and considerably faster. During the fight, he darted in and out, throwing lightning-quick jabs, eventually knocking his opponent down. For his part, Hemingway became infuriated at the referee, insisting that the latter had let the round go an extra three minutes.

But there would be no extra time added on here. There was no referee, no timekeeper. This was all out mayhem and there were no rules. Just the way I liked it. And I beat the living daylights out of Gracie, throwing numerous left jabs, a right hook, and a low blow for good measure, until the big man collapsed onto the canvas and pleaded with me to stop.

"Are you going to give me back my computer?"

"Yes, anything you want."

Much satisfied, I pulled the blanket up to my chin and fell fast asleep.

THE TRUTH SEEKER

Junk mail jammed up my mailbox until I received a note from the postman that unless I cleaned it out, no further mail would be delivered. I would have to travel to the post office to pick it up. I can't say I blamed the postman—the box was crammed and any more deliveries would have exploded it, I'm sure. It was just one of those mindless tasks that I disliked doing, sorting through trivial mail. All my bills came online and really, nobody sent me anything of importance via snail mail. It struck me that the senders of all this junk should have to clean out my mailbox, but I realized this was not going to happen.

I filled a plastic bag with the dross and made my way back to my apartment, dumping the entire lot onto the kitchen table. Nothing, nothing—mostly an endless array of food flyers ... pizza, pasta, Chinese food ... But suddenly a newsletter caught my attention. It was taken out on the letterhead of a group called The Underclass and the message seemed to be devoted to a philosophy of sorts. Dime-store variety philosophy. I myself had a degree in philosophy, in the art of reasoning and wondering, and so could speak with authority. Still, the newsletter piqued my interest.

"The world is run by psychopaths fueled by greed," it was written. "Bankers, lawyers, stockbrokers, investors, venture capitalists. Money-grubbing pigs. They play power games, manufacture weapons, and by carrying a large footprint, divest the world of its resources. They are interested in one thing and one thing only: accumulating as much wealth for themselves as possible. In earlier times they were considered 'robber barons'. But is the term any less apt today? They exploit the underclass for their own gain by paying nominal wages, enslaving those in need. They drive small companies out of business and build monopolies. They are today's counterparts to the medieval German feudal lords who charged exorbitant fees on ships to traverse the Rhine River. This country, this world, needs a cleansing. We need to clean out all the capitalists and not give them sympathy."

I flipped through the thin newsletter, eight pages in all. All the articles were anti-capitalist rants. Diatribes against big business, oil barons, and the very wealthy. One quoted Karl Marx, citing capitalism as being the "dictatorship of the ..." There was verbiage about the oppression of the exploited working class—the proletariat, the wage slaves, the workers alienated from the fruits of their own labour.

I wondered how this newsletter made it into the mail. Maybe I shouldn't have been surprised—I had, on occasion, received other communist rags. Moreover, I had heard this type of "philosophy" a million times before. While it always made some sense on a grassroots level, I discarded it. The fact of the matter was that, despite the ascent to power of certain money-hungry individuals, no other economic system in the world had ever worked. Certainly not communism, which is what Marx espoused. Besides, I had studied true philosophers like Georg Hegel and Friedrich Nietzsche in depth and so couldn't abide by this pseudo-philosophy. It was too easy ... extractions from Marxist doctrine manipulated and chopped into palatable bites for the unsuspecting twenty-first century masses. Ted Kaczynski, the Unabomber, had a similar manifesto that was all drivel. Thirty-five thousand words that called for a worldwide revolution against the effects of society's industrial-technological system. The guy should have stuck to the mathematics he was schooled in.

The one thing that struck a deep chord in me was that one article in the newsletter culminated with a paragraph that read: "Do not be afraid to take what is rightly yours. Beat the pigs at their own game. Steal when you can, what you can. You have the right."

I sat at the kitchen table, appraising the damage such a doctrine could have on someone, especially someone vulnerable. If you felt overwhelmed by life and this newsletter ended up on your doorstep, or rather in your mailbox, then reading these words might fuel the notion that the world was inherently unfair and that you deserved better. You might be tempted to actually "steal when you can." Become a shoplifter. A thief.

I decided I would find out exactly who The Underclass was. I felt that they should be made aware of how damaging their words could be. It was one thing to put out misleading flyers spouting all sorts of nonsense, but quite another to have that material fall into the wrong hands.

I found them easily enough in a small office above an Afghan carpet store on St. Clair Avenue. The wooden stairs creaked beneath the weight of my feet and sure enough, there before me, on the third floor adjacent to a weight loss clinic, was the front door for The Underclass, Inc. A sign said to take off your shoes so I carried them through the chiming door. No one was at the front desk, which was piled high with Underclass flyers and news-letters. Next to the flyers was an open box of donuts from Tim Hortons. And next to that a bell. *Please ring*, the sign next to the bell said. So I did.

A man came shuffling out of the back room. "Yes, can I help you?" he said.

I pulled out the newsletter I had brought.

"Is this your work?" I asked.

He took the flyer from my hands and read through it. "Yes, obviously it's from our organization."

"And can I ask you what sort of organization you actually are?"

"You can, but I'm not necessarily going to answer you. I don't even know who you are."

We were at a standoff—he didn't know who I was and I sure as hell didn't know who The Underclass was. I surveyed the wretch of an individual standing before me. He was in his late forties or fifties, with only a smat-tering of fine wispy hair, and an ample girth that ex-tended out his ill-fitting shirt and over his belt. The dark sweat from his armpits was clearly visible against the white of the shirt. I summed him up in one word—*failure*.

I quickly understood that if I told the truth about why I was there, that the guy would clam right up. So I lied.

"I found your newsletter in my mailbox and uh, thought I might be interested in joining your group. I'm curious what you have to offer."

The Failure looked at me quizzically. "Really? You want to know what we're about, what we espouse? Didn't you read the newsletter? That's exactly what we're all about. It's all there."

I chuckled. "You know, I'm just a student. Mature student, but still. Smart, but you know us academics, a bit scatterbrained. Need to be spoon-fed information. And the truth is …" Here I hesitated.

"Yes, the truth is … what?"

"Well, the truth is I'd like to know what the truth is. There's so much misinformation in the media these days, I don't know who's telling the truth."

The Failure took a seat behind the mahogany desk and told me to take my own chair.

"You know anything about philosophy?" he said. "Like Marx and Engels?"

"Not much. I think they were commies, right? You know, I took an undergraduate course once in philosophy but that was ages ago." I motioned with a sweep of my hand over my head that the material had been above me anyway.

"No worries. I can fill you in. What's your name anyway?"

"Joseph," I lied. "Joseph Briden."

The Failure extended a hand across the desk. "Michael Watson. Good to meet you, Joseph." He grabbed a jelly donut from the box and placed it on the desk in front of him. "Hope you don't mind. I haven't had lunch yet. Can I offer you one?"

"Sure." I selected a chocolate glaze and gently squeezed. The thing was stale, hard as a rock.

"Coffee?"

"Great. Two sugars, no cream."

While Michael went to get the coffees, I held the newsletter out in front of me. "It says here that you should *Steal when you can, what you can. You have the right.* Is that what you believe?"

"We sure do," Michael said confidently, handing me my mug. He settled into his seat and took a bite of his donut. Blue congealed jelly slipped onto his hand that he promptly lapped up with his tongue. "Ever hear of that old adage, *Cheaters never prosper*?"

"Of course."

"It's not true. Cheaters and liars do prosper. In fact, those are the people who run society."

"They run society, huh?" If I was to get anything from the fat pig sitting in front of me, I knew I had to play as dumb as possible.

"Yup. And they're psychopaths. Psychopaths are the heads of corporations, political and military leaders, you name it. They have their filthy hands in everything. The only difference between a psychopath who kills people and the ones who run companies is self-control. Killers are very impulsive. Corporate moguls aren't. But they're both the same. Both the same." Michael reflected on those last three words as if he were sipping a fine cognac. His eyes closed languidly and he took a deep breath.

"So what about the stealing part?" I said, returning to the question I had posed.

"The psychopaths have direct control over all the assets. But they didn't earn them; they stole them from the people." Michael used his index finger to point to his chest. "From people like me. So by stealing, you're only taking back what rightly belongs to you."

"And uh, what are the characteristics of these people?"

"Good question, Joseph. I'll tell you. First, they're all high achievers. Oh sure, they get things done but they leave people strewn in their wake. People are nothing more than commodities for them. Chattel. And very disposable." Michael went on to say that these people were able to work their way up the food chain because they were not only ruthless and devious, but charming as well. "No one can resist a charmer," he said, sighing. "They're the best actors." Vladimir Putin, Pol Pot, Charles Manson, Leonarda Cianciulli, Idi Amin, Henry VIII—according to Michael, they all displayed psychopathic behaviour. He went on to name many others, CEOs of Fortune 500 Companies, famous politicians, military leaders. A toxic brew of predators that had no regard for anyone other than themselves.

I had heard of them all but not Leonarda Cianciulli. I asked him about her.

"She was known as the Soap-Maker of Correggio," Michael said. "She was the most famous of Italian serial killers. Between 1939 and 1940, she murdered three women and made them into soap."

"What kind of soap?" I said, laughing.

"Ha. Good one again, Joseph. I don't know what sort of soap. But I can tell you that she took the leftover blood from her victims and mixed it with flour, sugar, chocolate, milk, eggs, a few other ingredients, and kneaded the dough into tea cakes, which she served to her neighbours. A true psychopath."

"That's really sick," I said.

"Well, that's what you can get when you deal with these type of people," Michael said. "They take great pleasure in the misfortunes of others. They plunder and pillage others for their own gain. Given a choice, they would rather plagiarize and steal than do an honest day's labour. And you know, they can't be rehabilitated. Their pathology is hardwired into their genes."

The funny thing is that after listening to Michael's diatribe, I didn't necessarily disagree with what he had said. He was still a lowlife in my books, but did have some valid points.

"So how do you survive?"

"You mean *me* personally?"

"No, I mean your organization."

"Donations. We have a lot of support. A lot."

I was now more intrigued with Michael. *A lot of support?* I wasn't surprised. People were naïve, drinking cyanide-laced, grape-flavoured Kool-Aid à la Jim Jones. Following modern day faith healers like Jim Bakker whose only supernatural powers involved lining their own pockets without anyone catching on. Still, the fact that Michael had that support *and* made some sense was an interesting mix. Nonetheless, I wanted to move the conversation away from psychopathic behaviour back to my home field, back to philosophy. Then I would expose him for the cad he was.

"So Michael, just getting back to that Marx and Engels stuff, are you a communist?"

"I hate labels. So no, I'm not. But if you're asking me whether I know about their philosophy, I can tell you that I read the *Communist Manifesto* many times."

So had I. Little did he know.

"Marx may have been wrong about communism because he didn't foresee the tyranny that enslaved Eastern

Europe and the old Soviet Union," Michael said. "But he was spot-on when it came to capitalism. I'm sure I don't have to tell you that the middle-class is vanishing in this country. In many countries. Communism used the practice of a centralized economic management and redistribution of income. Of course there were problems of abuse. There was no equality. The *Manifesto* talked about overthrowing the bourgeoisie and allowing political power to be managed by the proletariat. It didn't happen. The question becomes, is capitalism any better?"

Michael took another bite of his donut, ripping it off with his teeth, and a long sip from his coffee. Good, he was collecting himself. Soon I would pull apart his ideas and the massacre would begin. I had heard all the arguments, both sides. Why Marx had it right. Why Marx had it wrong.

"Do you want to know why Marx wanted the proletariat to have political power?" Michael said in between bites.

I didn't want to go there. It all had to do with avoiding the worker alienation that Michael and company had written about in the newsletter. Have the proletariat overthrow the capitalist system of private property, have them share the wealth they produced through a communist economic system, and, like the proverbial rabbit popping out of a magician's hat, interest in one's own labour would be restored. I didn't need Michael to lecture me on all that.

"Nah," I said, waving my hand over my head as I had done earlier. "Just tell me about why capitalism stinks."

"Ok, let's talk about that. But first, I've noticed that you haven't eaten your donut."

I looked skeptically at the hard shell that I held gingerly in my hand. Under no circumstance would I take a bite.

"I'm saving it for later. Mind if I take it with me?"

"Here, have the whole box," Michael said, flipping the lid shut and passing it to me.

I pushed it back at Michael. "Oh, no, no thank you," I said. "I'm trying to cut back. Too much sugar."

"Huh. That'd odd. Nothing wrong with sugar in my opinion."

"You might be right. Makes everything taste better, that's for sure." I reached for the box of donuts. "Ok, I'll take them."

Michael licked his lips and nodded. "Under our capitalist society," he said, "big business today is said not to be concentrated in the hands of a few. These aren't feudal times, right?" He laughed. "Some people say that because you can … get this … buy common shares in those big businesses. You can own a piece of the pie. Isn't that nice?"

Michael banged his fist onto the desk, creating a small tsunami of coffee waves that nearly escaped his cup. "It's not true!" he yelled, the veins in his neck looking like they were about to burst. "The concentration of economic power is still in the hands of a few. Tell me, how many people, ordinary people, do you know that own shares in corporations?"

I didn't know any, but then, I knew very few people.

"The fact of the matter is that there are not many possibilities these days for poor men to become rich men. Even middle-class men. Students are coming out of university saddled with mounds of debt; job security is non-existent. Even if you have a job, very few have defined-benefit pension plans anymore."

The quizzical look on my face didn't escape Michael's attention.

"So, let me explain the defined-benefit pension plan," he said. "At the end of your working days, you know exactly how much money you'll have in that pension. Defined-contribution, and you don't. Your pension is governed by market forces. But just try and earn a good interest rate on your capital these days. You can't. Prices of goods and services are rising all the time and in effect, your capital is being eroded."

Michael wasn't finished. He asked me for my impressions of the 2008 financial debacle.

I shrugged my shoulders.

"In 2008, stock markets around the world crashed. In the U.S., thousands upon thousands of people defaulted on their mortgages because the value of their homes tanked; they were now worth much less than their outstanding mortgages." Michael went on to talk about credit default swaps, reckless lending practices by big banks, subprime mortgages, and how the big companies were complicit in all this. I knew nothing about any of this, only vaguely having recalled the incident. Why would I? Just as I had no money now, I had no money then. There was nothing on the line for me; it was just another news story.

"And the worst part," Michael said, "is that not one CEO associated with the biggest banks and insurance companies has ever been arrested."

"Well, you would need some proof," I said. "You can't just stand in front of a judge and say, 'Hey Your Honour, throw the book at this guy for causing a market melt-down.'" It was a low blow, a groin punch, and I knew it would rile Michael up. I felt a little undermanned talking about all this financial stuff and wanted to even out the playing hand. It did the trick. He gritted his teeth and furrowed his brow. For a second, I thought he would create another tsunami. But much to my surprise, he maintained his composure.

"There is proof," he stated emphatically, grimacing. "But it's covered up. Everyone at the top is involved. The Feds, Justice Department, the banks, insurance companies … no one will squeal on anyone else because they all grease each other's palms." Michael sighed and the tone of his voice cranked down a notch or two. "People are tired of getting shafted, Joseph. They're tired of seeing the psychopaths at the top get away with murder. Everyone's fed up. That's why the Occupy movement started in 2011. It was a worldwide protest movement against social and economic disparity."

I could see Michael was tired of talking. Maybe he was simply tired of fighting the battle. I felt for him. He wasn't such a bad guy, after all. So I shifted the conversation once again, throwing him a softball.

"And you said you have lectures, right?"

"Usually once a month."

"Large turnout?"

"The last lecture there were over four hundred. We scrambled to find some extra seats."

I lowered my head and stared at the newsletter, lost in thought.

"Anything else, Joseph?"

"No, I guess not."

Michael stood up, signaling the end of the conversation. I noticed he had his shoes on. "Well, I hope to see you at the next meeting," he said, clapping me on the back like we were now long-lost friends finally getting back together. "You'll find many truths there. That's what we're all about."

I put my shoes back on and, as I walked down the steps and out the door, broke into a run. I just wanted to get as far away as I could from the place I had just been. My expectations were all wrong—I had been anticipating some punk, an anarchist without a single brain cell in his deluded head. Someone with a basket full of puffball ideas between the ears that I could easily pull apart like taffy. Instead I got Michael, a slob, but a coherent one. Someone whose logic I couldn't take issue with. No holes from what I could discern. I hadn't said a single thing that I had intended—not that he, Michael, was a piece of shit, not that The Underclass flyers might contribute to the demise of people, not that the message was inferior philosophy. Not a single bloody word.

Running empty on fumes, I stopped in a Jamaican patty store and took a seat.

"What'll it be, mon?" the waiter asked. He had dreadlocks down to his waist and was wearing a colourful knit cap.

"Two beef patties. Mild. And a Coke."

"Spicy ones might be better," he said. "You look like you can use a lift. Spice up! Good for all dat ails you."

Wow, he got it. Maybe because I was holding my head like it weighed too much for my neck, my chin resting between the palms of my hands.

"I don't know."

"Need a talk, mon? My name is Jacko."

"You always so friendly?"

"That's me. Master patty maker, friend to all in need."

"Well, the thing is, Jacko, I went looking for the truth today. I always thought I knew what it was. Now I'm not sure. I don't know what to believe anymore."

"Well, my friend," Jacko said, "the truth is only what you believe. Nuthin' more." He thumped at his chest with a closed fist. "If you feel it here, in you heart, dat's the truth. And everybody has der own version. Der's no one truth in dis here world."

"That's what the truth is, huh?"

"Yup. Dat's what it is."

I nodded slowly and lifted my head up so my eyes met with Jacko's. "Ok, two spicy beef patties."

REJECTION

s far as I knew, not a single person in the city cared that I was a bona-fide philosopher. To them, I was nothing less than a trickster, a crazed magician of sorts, able to bend spoons with only my words. Manipulating those words until they wrapped around their frazzled brains. Until I got my point across, crystallizing my ideas. I had read that philosophers in a couple of overseas London bars were sometimes employed to engage patrons in conversation—philosophical conversations—presumably to keep those patrons drinking. Well, at least they found employment. But here, no one cared. No one.

Worst of all were the women, who rejected me like I was a leper. I could never make any headway with them. I had had a few relationships over the years, but they all faded, the women leaving, ghosting me. Women offered pleasure but instilled fear, which I could not shake. My uncertainty about self-image, career choice, money, goals —those drove a wedge between me and my lovers. I just couldn't risk being judged. So university became my haven, philosophy my mistress. It was better that way. Much easier than getting involved with women. Affairs of the heart were not the *sine qua non* of my world. On the one occasion when I did let someone in for a longer look-see, it was an unmitigated disaster. Michelle Lambert was an English major that I met in the school's cafeteria. I was enchanted with her looks as well as her smarts, but we ended up arguing all the time. Probably on account of those very smarts, she wouldn't acquiesce to my own intellect and we seemed to one-up each other all the time. She would lift an incredulous eye above the rim of her glasses whenever I said something she disagreed with, and I knew then I was in for a major fight. If I said Dostoyevsky was a great writer, she would say Dickens was better. Or if she talked about Robert Browning, I would say that poets were simply writers who didn't know how to write prose. You see what I mean? One-upping each other. These arguments, which I never did win, served to fracture my straight and purposeful resolve, leaving me limp with anger.

As a result of being rejected, I felt no connection to anyone, especially to women. It was like I was an alien just landed. If I could have lived in a cave at the side of a mountain, I would have done so. Then one day I thought: *Why not? Why not leave the city for a time and live off the land?* I really needed a vacation from my life. So I took a bus to an area roughly three hours north of Toronto, where the terrain was especially hilly. How did I know where to go? Simple, I Googled it.

Having slept poorly the night before, I was already tired when I boarded the bus. I read a book of short stories by Gabriel García Marquez during the trip and seemingly in no time flat, the bus opened its doors and let me out. The rain, which had accompanied us throughout the trip, streaking the windows, had not let up. As soon as I debarked, I was pelted with water and the wind whipped my face. The other two people who left the bus, a middle-aged couple, immediately ran into a building and so I was left alone in the middle of a dirt road. I hiked up my backpack, filled with fruit, three bottles of water, some wine, and sandwiches, and started to walk out of the godforsaken little village that was in the middle of nowhere. On top of my backpack was a rolled up sleeping bag, one that I had once purchased at a garage sale but never used. With my eyes stinging, my glasses runny with water, it was nearly impossible to see. I squinted and noticed hills in the distance. That was my destination, why not?

I put one heavy foot in front of the other. And the longer I walked, the greater the incline became. Although I couldn't make out my surroundings, there was no question but that I was walking uphill. Each step was an effort and it was like I was trudging through a bowl of Jell-O. My shoes became muddy and I was soaked through and through. Every few minutes I stopped to try and get some bearings, but it was no use ... I couldn't see even two feet in front. When finally the rain abated somewhat, I found myself standing close to a gaggle of Holstein cows. Chewing their cud, they stared at me as though I were insane. And maybe I was. A city boy born and raised, standing in the middle of a farmer's field. I had wandered off the main path. I made a face, sticking my tongue out and opening my eyes wide as saucers, but except for a solitary "moo," there was no response from the animals. Cold and miserable, I squeezed some water from my hair and then cut a swath through knee-high grass, jumping a small barbed wired fence.

I shivered uncontrollably but found that if I picked up the pace, I felt somewhat better. I had not jogged my entire life, but there I was, sliding over the terrain like a long-distance runner. So I continued jogging and scanned the countryside where I might bed down for the night. The sun was setting and I needed to rest ... all this exercise. It occurred to me then that perhaps I had made a grievous mistake. The question I thought of was evident to even the simplest minds: What exactly was I doing in this remote region, surrounded by farmers' fields and grazing cows, when I had my own bed in the city?

There was no one around, of that I was fairly certain. I had read that this area was prime hiking territory but at this time of year, newly removed from the dreaded winter and still quite chilly, not to mention muddy, it was only rarely traversed. I veered from the dirt road I was walking on and proceeded to my left, where I began to climb over sheer rock face. I could have stayed on the dirt road, but no, that was too easy. And "easy" had never been part of my world. My wet shoes slipped time and again as I scaled upward on hands and feet, sending a small avalanche of gravelly rock downward. Fortunately, the incline wasn't all that steep and I was in no danger of falling.

And then I found it. A cave. Well, sort of. Not the deep limestone type that one studies in high school geography class, full of stalactites and stalagmites hanging from the ceiling like icicles. Hardly, it was more like a shallow burrow dug by some large animal, a bear perhaps, and only a few metres deep. But for my purposes, it was perfect. A place to bed down.

I removed two peanut-butter-and-strawberry-jam sandwiches from my backpack and sat down on the dirt floor of my cave to have dinner. I was famished and ate quickly, gobbling up the food. I wasn't exactly warm—my wet clothing stuck like a second skin to my body—but at least I was protected from the elements. It was still spitting rain and as I looked down into the valley below, I could make out a solitary fox scampering along a hill.

After swilling down the remnants of a bottle of wine, I let out a long sigh and my body relaxed. This wasn't so bad after all. The view was good, the company fine, and best of all was that nobody knew where I was. I could assume a second, inconspicuous life—Karl Pringle, Earth Man. I rolled out my sleeping bag to let it dry and stayed sitting for hours, doing absolutely nothing but gazing into the distance and looking at the rain, which had picked up once again.

But then a strange thing happened. The longer I stayed stock-still, the more my brain started to wander. And it dawned on me that I had indeed made a fine mess of my life, that I was a major fuck-up … I had no job, no prospects, no friends, and very little money. I sighed and my chest constricted. And as the sun had now completely receded and I was awash in blackness, I was suddenly overcome with loneliness. Abject solitude that was unremitting and that bore down and covered me like a shroud. I had to lie down. I carried the still-damp sleeping bag toward the interior of the cave and slipped between the covers, pulling my legs into a fetal position, my body shivering, and hands beneath my head. I could hear the rain falling and was very glad for the sound. It lulled me to sleep.

In the morning, after sleeping surprisingly well, I woke with a burning desire to empty my bowels. The ground was saturated with dew and the rays of the sun shone brightly. Birds soared overhead in lazy swoops. As I left the cave and veered off onto the main path, I could see the cows grazing peacefully down below in the pasture where I had been. The chimney of the farmhouse was billowing lazy grey smoke. I saw a couple of black squirrels and felt incredibly energized by the entirety of my surroundings ... any doubts I had had about what I was doing in the countryside were now gone. I felt that much better after I relieved myself in a wooded area. Only then did it occur to me that I had forgotten to bring toilet paper. So I reached down for some withered brown leaves from the ground and did the best I could. Then I used water from one of the bottles for a thorough wash. Not a great job then but what the heck, there was no one around.

I hung my sleeping bag and clothes from tree branches to dry out and returned to my cave to have breakfast. Another couple of sandwiches, this time baloney and ham with sliced tomatoes, and a healthy bunch of carrot and celery slices. Sitting there in my underwear, I felt considerably better than the previous night. Looking down at the valley, I noticed railroad tracks, a smattering of farmer's fields, and in the distance, the small village where the bus had dropped me off. After the long winter, I could smell the impending renewal of nature, with vegetation inching through the soil. It was an "earthy" sort of smell; there was no other way to describe it. A smell of mud, grass, tree bark, leaves and dew.

Then my eye caught sight of something glinting in the sunlight. I descended carefully from my perch and walked over. Hidden behind a phalanx of fallen branches was a very small cast iron charcoal grill. Undoubtedly left by campers, the discovery left me dumbfounded. There were briquettes of some sort in the grill; I had seen ones made of charcoal before but these looked curiously like peat moss. There was a small crack in the grill but I didn't care.

I carried my find back to the cave and searched my knapsack for the lighter I always carried with me. I tried lighting the briquettes; they sparked but wouldn't catch hold, there was too much moisture.

Moving away from the cave, I upturned the grill and laid out the briquettes next to a tree where they could dry. The sun was shining brightly and I knew in a few hours all the dampness would be gone.

I grabbed hold of a low-lying tree branch and let out a little shriek as I hung. Just because I could. A train then rumbled by and I hid behind a tree. I was still in my underwear and peeked out, venturing a wave with my right hand. A short, Queen-like wave. Nothing ostentatious. Ok, so maybe I wasn't exactly like the Queen of England. Or the King. But this was my space now, and I lorded over it.

Days passed and I began to run out of food. Only a couple of sandwiches remained. I considered returning home but liked being out in the country by myself so much that I decided against it. Sure things were rough, like no change of clothes, no food, no toilet paper, no shower ... but with the exception of the food, those were all minor inconveniences.

I watched a rabbit hop on by and thought about how tasty it might be. I could kill the little varmint and roast it. By this time, the peat had dried and I found I could easily light it. So I had a stove. All that was missing was something to fry up.

I decided right then that I might as well have a decent meal. So I followed the little rabbit into a forested area, where I lay low behind a boulder. He was cute, I had to admit, but it didn't matter—now it was all about survival.

I stayed behind the boulder until the rabbit moved into the shadows of the trees, a tangle of intertwined limbs that leaned heavily toward me, obscuring my vision. If I didn't know better, I would have thought they were protecting the rabbit. I stood up, had a look behind some trees and not seeing any sign of the hopping critter, retreated back to my cave.

The next morning I woke to the sounds of something rummaging through my knapsack. A wolf! All black, with streaks of tangled auburn fur down its back, it was now eating the last of my peanut-butter-and-jam sandwiches. I lay still, not daring to move. If it was a wolf, I might be next on its menu. I suddenly thought the better of remaining quiet; perhaps doing so wasn't the best idea. I didn't know though … this was nature, and really, what did I know about nature? I may have been the Earth Man but that was a sham, I was clearly out of my depths.

I decided on the spur of the moment that I would let the intruder know I was in charge. The alpha male. Perhaps that was best. I was about to yell out when the animal slowly made its way over to me and put its cold nose up against mine. Christ. I closed my eyes, my heart beat wildly, and waited for the worst. But then it licked my face ... once ... twice. I opened my eyes and saw that the creature had rolled onto its back, its legs sticking straight up into the air. I took a chance and started rubbing the belly. Would a wolf really ask for a belly rub? As little as I knew about nature, I concluded that probably not, that this had to be a dog.

I could feel every rib; this was one skinny pooch.

"Hey, you," I said, "who do you belong to?"

I got onto my knees and patted the dog's fur, my hand getting stuck in the burrs. "You need a bath, Mister."

The dog, who had the appearance of a medium-sized mutt, closed its eyes meaningfully upon the remark and resumed licking my face. Its tongue felt like sandpaper.

When I had had enough face licks, I gently pushed the dog away. Its spindly appendages unable to maintain the weight of its body, it quickly dropped onto the ground like a stone and lay at my feet. It needed a lot more food than peanut butter sandwiches.

"I think you've been on your own a long time," I said. "Just like me. I wonder if you have a name, huh?"

The dog opened its mouth as if to speak and I fondled its snout.

"How about I call you *Gorky*? You kind of look like a Gorky to me."

I dressed and walked down to the railroad tracks, Gorky managed to stand up and follow close behind, doing his best to keep up. Another train passed, I lowered my pants and mooned it. *What did I care? There was nothing wrong with doing that ... who hadn't seen a bum before?* Then I skedaddled back up the hill to the cave and hid deep inside, shivering with excitement; I really was free to do anything I wanted.

"I know this might seem strange to you, Gorky," I said, "but I'm a free spirit and I do exactly as I please. You have no problem with that, right?"

Gorky let out a tiny yip.

"Thought so."

My stomach was rumbling and I suspected so was Gorky's. I made a half-hearted attempt to look for the rabbit, but it was nowhere to be seen. Having a mangy dog at my side was certainly a detriment to catching something to eat. More than likely Gorky would have wanted to play with anything I tried to catch.

There were plenty of squirrels scampering about but I wasn't about to eat one. They looked like giant rats. Gross. But at a little creek I found half a dozen green frogs lazily reposing on a rock, basking in the sun. I took my shoe off and bonked them, one after another. Again and again until they were flattened out, Gorky looking on passively. I scooped the pieces to the grill and started the briquettes up, searing the food, blood and every-thing else, until it was all crisp and golden. Then I ate it, tentatively at first, but then with gusto. It was actually pretty good, tasting much like chicken. I handed a chunk to Gorky, who gobbled it down.

I was still hungry, so I went looking for the rabbit. But again the little bastard was nowhere to be found. So I thought I would check out the farmer's field—surely he had chickens or roosters. I put on all my clothes and Gorky and I walked back down the path until we came to the barbed wire fence that I had previously jumped. I carefully lifted Gorky over and cautiously slid between rungs of the wire. We walked past a dozen cows but our presence didn't faze them at all. Gorky, though, started fidgeting, rearing up on his hind legs.

"You have to be quiet here," I said. And it struck me at that instant that Gorky had never barked. He had let out a single yip, but not a bark. Not once.

Just as I suspected, there was a chicken coop near the house and, when we entered through the wooden doors of the barn, fowl flew hither and yon, their feathers fluttering into the stale air. I set my sights on the smallest of the bunch and while Gorky sat on his haunches and watched, I made a lunge for it. It squirmed madly in my arms and tried to peck at me.

"Piece of shit!"

So I wrung its neck. A quick twist and it was all over, the thing fell dead in my arms. I opened the barn doors and stuck my head out. Gorky did likewise. When I was sure no one was around, we made a mad dash back to the fence and then up the path to my hideout. I looked for a rock with a sharp edge and proceeded to remove the chicken feathers as best I could. Blood squirted everywhere but after a few minutes, I had in my hands some semblance of a chicken we might eat. All I had to do was fry it up. I lit the peat and blew on it until red hot embers appeared. Then I carefully laid the bird onto the grill and with Gorky following at my heels, walked back to the creek to wash myself.

***

Every day after that, Gorky and I snuck into the barn where I proceeded to steal a bird. Some days two. And sometimes even eggs. On one occasion someone came in and Gorky and I hid behind a bale of hay. My heart beat madly and only when the barn door closed was I able to breathe again. Good ol' Gorky ... he just kept watch and not a whisper came from his mouth—he was the perfect foil.

Unnerved by the episode, Gorky and I didn't return to the barn but instead scoured the countryside for something to eat. I found more frogs and killed an entire colony without a thought. I also found some berries on bushes.

"These might be poisonous," I said. "What do you think, Gork?" I held a handful in my palm and let my companion sniff them. Gorky licked his lips and that was good enough for me. We gobbled them up. My big find that day, however, was the bunny that had to this point eluded me. I saw it hop behind a boulder and ran after it. I bent onto my haunches and reached into my pocket, pulling out some berries that I held in my open hand. Unbelievably, it crept forward. It didn't seem at all scared. I couldn't believe it. I slowly picked up a large rock with my free hand and brought it down hard on the animal's head. There was a loud crunch and the thing dropped dead at my feet. For good measure, I whacked it a couple of more times, dismembering one of the legs. Gorky stood passively throughout, looking on in awe.

I brought the rabbit back to the grill where I skinned it. There wasn't much peat moss left to light so I used twigs and some pages from the Marquez book I had brought along. It took hours to cook through but, when the meat was almost a toasty golden brown, Gorky and

I ate heartily. I couldn't believe a rabbit could taste that good. I licked my fingers and, when I saw Gorky licking his chops, I laughed out loud.

I sat back against one wall of the cave and with the back of my head firmly cradled within my open palms, my companion's head in my lap, I considered that things were very good indeed. It had now been ten days since my adventure began and I was in a much better frame of mind than when I left the city. I even thought that perhaps I could extend the vacation for quite some time, weeks, months maybe.

The next day, bright and early, I took handfuls of berries and with Gorky at my side, waited patiently for the train I knew would be coming. It arrived regularly and when it passed, the sound of the rail cars clacking in my ears, I reared back and flung the berries at the windows. They landed with splats. I could see passengers pointing at me and I dropped my pants to reveal my backside once again. Screw them. Were they so much better than me? I should hardly think not.

We trudged back up the hill and I got myself together, washing in the creek. The time seemed right to pay a visit to the village. I drank some of the water and then cleaned up Gorky as best I could, using my wet comb to smooth his fur. Gorky shook all over like an outboard motor revving up. Then we slowly walked back down the hill to the little village.

"You and me, Gork. You and me. We're not going anywhere yet, but soon."

In a convenience store I bought some dried pepperoni, cheese, rye bread, olives, paper plates, water, and a large bag of kibble.

"New in town?" the storekeeper asked.

"Just camping out with my trusty companion here."

I looked awful, I'm sure, and I smelled. So what? People accepted you more readily when you had a dog, and the storekeeper threw in two cans of dog food.

"Promotional giveaway," he said.

"Thanks. Very nice of you."

Back at the cave, Gorky and I settled down to enjoy our feast. I had never seen an animal eat like that ... no sooner did I finish filling a plate with kibble than Gorky gobbled it all and looked up at me with doleful eyes. The poor kid, he had probably gone weeks, months maybe, without having anything substantial to chow down on. To spice things up for him, I added bits of cheese and pepperoni into his food.

As a habit, after a meal Gorky and I would go for a walk. I would sometimes throw a stick for him to fetch but he never did chase after it; it was painfully obvious that he had never learned to play. What a shame.

*　*　*

The lure of more eggs and chickens was too strong and I decided it was time for another visit to the farmer's field. An intoxicating smell of warming strawberry pie wafted to my nostrils. I could see Gorky sniffing the air as well. We bypassed the barn and instead made a bee-line to the stone house, where the smell was coming from. I stood on tiptoes and looked in through the open window. There they were, a couple of pies cooling on the wooden kitchen table.

"Smells nice, huh Gork?" I whispered. "Bet they taste even better."

There was no one in the kitchen and I thought that, if I opened the window just a bit more, I might be able to sneak in and grab them. I slipped my fingers underneath the window sill and began to push the window more fully open. Suddenly, I could hear a woman's voice and I started at the sound.

"Can I help you?"

It wasn't exactly a question. Not really. It was more like an accusation, one tinged with rancour. I readily accepted that, I wasn't about to make excuses, especially as I saw the woman standing with a pitchfork in hand. She wore a blue kerchief around her head, worn jeans, and around her waist, a flowered apron.

"Me and my dog here, we're just hungry," I said. With that pronouncement, Gorky walked over to the woman, his ears pinned back and his tail forming little concentric circles in the air.

"Well, this here dog is sure skin and bones," the woman said, stroking Gorky's fur. "You been stealing our chickens, haven't you?"

"Yes."

"Come inside."

She lowered the pitchfork and opened the front door. Gorky and I followed through the threshold into a large and inviting living room, a fire glowing in the cast iron hearth.

"Have a seat."

Still nervous, I tried to make myself comfortable in a wooden rocking chair. Gorky, ever obedient, sat at my feet. The woman, who I took to be in her late fifties, perhaps older, remained standing, the pitchfork still in her hands.

"Now then," she said, her dark eyes giving me the once-over like I was a common criminal, "how do you intend to pay me back for all the chickens and eggs you stole?"

I took out my wallet and offered her everything inside, a grand total of $28.35.

"Do you know how much each chicken costs?"

"No idea."

Just then, a calico cat wandered into the living room and, upon seeing Gorky, arched its back menacingly. Gorky simply watched the feline with searching eyes but didn't move.

"Her name's Rapunzel. And what's your dog's name?"

"I don't know. He's not exactly my dog. He just came into my little camp and has been hanging around. I call him Gorky."

"Gorky? That's a strange name for a dog."

"There was a writer by the same name."

"I have no time for reading," the woman said.

I could smell the sweet aroma of the pies and it made me salivate.

"And what's your name?" the woman asked.

"Karl. Karl Pringle."

"Well, Karl Pringle, I'm Hilda. We don't get many strangers around here this time of year and when we do, and if they want to rest their bones, we let them stay a night or two. But when they steal from us, that there's a different story . . ."

"I was hungry, that's all," I said. "I'm sorry. I didn't mean you any harm. I came from the city and didn't bring enough food with me. I'm really not used to camping out. And you know, I wanted Gorky to have some food."

"You coulda knocked on the door, all friendly like, and me or my husband Morty woulda helped you out."

"Where is your husband?" I wasn't sure if this was an appropriate question or not but out it came all the same. I leaned forward toward the hearth and rubbed my hands vigorously; they were cold and stiff .

"Buying some livestock at an auction. He won't be back until late."

"Anyway, I have money back in the city," I said. "I can send it to you when I get back to Toronto."

The offer seemed to satisfy Hilda. She asked whether I was hungry, didn't wait for an answer, and ushered me into the kitchen. Gorky followed and ignored the swipe Rapunzel took at his rear end.

Pots and pans hung from hooks in the kitchen ceiling and the pies now looked as delicious as they smelled. Hilda fed both Gorky and myself large bowls of chicken stew from a cauldron that was on the stovetop and cut for me generous slices of black bread which I slathered with butter. The stew was brimming with chicken, potatoes, onions, carrots, peas—I had never tasted anything so exquisite and between mouthfuls, told Hilda that she was an amazing cook. She seemed to take great delight in watching me eat and as soon as I had finished one bowl, she said:

"Ready again?"

I nodded and very quickly my bowl was filled.

Hilda was a genuinely warm person. I don't know why, but she reminded me of my own mother. I hadn't thought of my deceased mother in a long time, mostly because doing so made me sad.

"Where are you camping out?" she asked, as she doled out a slice of strawberry pie. I was stuffed, which wasn't surprising given that I had had cheese, bread and pepperoni earlier that day. But the pie looked too good to pass up, the rich smell so alluring, I just had to indulge.

"In the hillside," I said in between mouthfuls. "I found a cave."

Hilda joined me for coffee, strong and black, with a dollop of brown sugar. It was just the right way to end the meal. I sat back, my belly sated, my mind at ease, my spirit relaxed. I looked down at Gorky. He had eaten three bowls of stew and was now curled up on the floor, sound asleep.

"You can stay here this night," said Hilda. "Normally if people want to bed down, we charge $45."

"Like a bed and breakfast."

"Exactly. We have plenty of room. But no one normally comes this time of year."

"I don't have that kind of money with me," I said.

"So if I let you stay, you'll owe for the chickens plus the room."

"That sounds fair. I can't complain."

"I'll show you your room," Hilda said. "You don't want to sleep outside any more—it's gloomy and damp this time of year."

"Very kind of you."

We let Gorky sleep it off on the floor and Hilda drew a bath for me. I never took baths, considered them a luxury I couldn't indulge in, and yet here I was, ready to slip into one.

"One bath for you and one for your dog," she said. "When he wakes I'm going to scrub him darned good. To get all the dirt off."

I stayed in that bath for a very long time, letting all the scum and grunge of the world dissolve. And when I emerged, Hilda had Gorky in his own bath out in a shed. Using a long-handled scrub brush, she untangled all of the messy fur. Water flew everywhere and a small puddle accumulated on the ground. Gorky remained silent throughout, looking down at the soapy water in resignation. I could see him anxiously swallowing and licking his lips, over and over.

"I don't really know how you got to be in such bad shape," Hilda said, "but from now on, you'll be looking like a respectable dog."

When the water had turned black as coal, Hilda lifted Gorky out of the tub and wrapped him in a big towel. She produced from her apron a treat of some sort that she let Gorky snatch from her palm. It worked—he appeared especially mollified at that point and if I didn't know better, I could have sworn that a smile creased his elongated face.

The cat, who had followed us from the main house, sat transfixed and only moved (with utter disdain) when Gorky gave himself a massive shake, spraying water everywhere.

We went back inside the house, and by this time, the sun was setting. I was glad to be inside this warm, inviting house; it was so much better than being outside and for once, I didn't mind the company. I even offered up some tidbits of a real conversation.

"I was in school a long time," I said, as I stretched out before the roaring hearth. "I should have worked, but I never knew what I could do. Really, the only thing I was good at was philosophy."

"Philosophy doesn't put bread and butter on your table. Only hard work does."

"Sounds logical."

'We were meant for work, in my opinion. You can take a rest in books or in your philosophy, but you should always return to work. It is a blessing. From the Lord. Ecclesiastes two, twenty-four says work has real value and rebukes sloth and idleness. You know what that word means, do you, Karl—*rebuke*? That there's one fancy world I know. Always have."

Oh my, bible stuff. But I knew better than to say even a single word. I just kept my mouth shut.

"So what are you doing now?" Hilda said.

"Nothing. No job. No blessing."

"Try to get some job using your hands. Maybe working the land. Working the land builds character. Builds up your constitution. That matters, son."

"I'll keep that in mind."

"You should. I know what I'm talking about. I'm no country bumpkin, you know."

"Those are words of wisdom."

"You're damn right they are."

I laughed. I wasn't sure what exactly Hilda was but a country bumpkin she wasn't. "So I'm going to leave in the morning," I said. "Go back to Toronto. And when I get there, I'll send you the money I owe."

"Keep your money," Hilda said. "But I think I should keep Gorky here. She'll have a lot of space to run around and Morty and me will make sure she's fed right proper."

"You mean ...?"

"Yes, we'll have to rename Gorky. Maybe *Jilly*. She's no boy."

"Wow. I had no clue."

"Trust me. I know."

And who was I to argue with her?

* * *

I never did meet Morty. By the time I woke and had breakfast of pancakes, scrambled eggs, and coffee, he was already hard at work driving a tractor. I looked out the kitchen window and Hilda pointed him out. There he was in the distance, a tiny speck against the horizon, partially obscured by the early-morning mist that arose from the field.

As I was about to leave, I put my arms around Gorky, rather *Jilly*, and gave her a hug. I didn't want to let go. She smelled so clean, and looked so happy. Never a peep from her, what a great dog. Tears streamed down my face. Hilda was right though—the dog was better off on the farm.

"Here, take this bag," Hilda said.

"What's that for?"

"Lunch. Meat and vegetables."

Hilda kissed my forehead and I embraced her. I embraced her, that was amazing! But she really was like my mother.

"I'll come back," I said.

"Come whenever you like. And remember what I said about work."

I walked out of there and waved as Hilda and Jilly stood in the doorway. I noticed all manner of equipment and tools leaning against the barn: rakes, a mower, sickles and shovels. I turned around to survey the countryside that had served me so well.

People on the bus going back to Toronto gave me a wide berth and no one sat next to me. I don't know why. I certainly didn't smell bad or anything like that. Even the driver looked at me as if I were some sort of farm animal.

So that's the way it's going to be, I thought. *Fine.*

But maybe it was just me imagining, I don't know. It didn't matter though, my trip to the countryside had been an unqualified success—it not only made me feel good that I could live off the land if I had to, but it also allowed me to figure things out. And the one unremitting conclusion I came up with was that, like I always said, it never ended well for me with females. If I liked them, they always left. Even Jilly.

EDNA

Being an unemployed philosopher has its advantages. You have a lot of time to muse about important things, like life and death. And since you're a thinking machine, it's the perfect pastime. There's also the fact that, if you're clever enough, you can devise ways that people will give you money for free. It only takes a little bit of ingenuity and a sign. For instance, if I'm strapped for cash, which is often the case, I'll sit on my decrepit rear end and beg for money. What could be better? It beats working.

***

I made a handy crude sign on a piece of torn cardboard:

PLEASE HELP. GIRLFRIEND DIED OF CANCER. ARMS HOLD NO ONE, HEART BROKEN. DEPRESSED. ANY SMALL CHANGE WILL DO.

I knew it would get attention, I know how to pull people's strings. *Arms that hold no one, a heart that is broken* ... of course, of course. People are so predictable, so malleable, I can always get away with it.

On most occasions, I set up shop in the St. Andrews subway station, the heart of the financial district. Four hours a day, during rush hour. When the suits come by, I press the door open for them. Their own personal butler. They stop to look at the sign, just as I know they will. Many drop coins into my Starbucks coffee cup and walk on, but a few stop to talk. To those who do linger, I tell a version of the truth, that my beloved is gone, dead. Cancer. It ravaged her once-beautiful body. It all became too much for me and I dropped out of the school where I had been a PhD candidate in philosophy. I had been doing TA work and was a rising star destined to become a prof. Now I'm a nothing, I tell anyone who'll listen.

"You're not *nothing*," various passersby say. "Just give it time."

I open my eyes wide and gaze upward gratefully, like I'm praying to my maker … hah! "Anything will do," I say. "You're so kind." I say that over and over again.

In no time at all, I have good coffee to drink, delicious muffins that people give me—banana, bran, blueberry. Sometimes even sandwiches—these I put in my backpack and keep for dinner. And the change, how it flows, plentiful manna from heaven. Of course, not everyone views my presence on the floor with equanimity.

"Get a job," I am sometimes told.

"I have one," I say. "I'm a beggar."

Better yet is this type of exchange: "You've made your own bed, your own choices that led you here. You have no one to blame but yourself."

And I shout after them, my words roiling through the subway halls: "Free will is an illusion! Things happen over which you have no control!" Then I shut up. I'm not about to engage in an argument about free will versus determinism. Or limited free will and limited determinism. I just want to make a point, to let the fools know I can't be bested, that I'm one smart dude. No one's fool. Not your ordinary vagrant.

Still, as crazy as it sounds, for perhaps the first time in my life, I feel somewhat content. Things have simplified and now, without my doing a thing, I am getting my just rewards. Why shouldn't I get things *just for being me?* I'm so much brighter than most, gifted. A philosopher's job is only to consider the nature of being, not to teach English to foreigners, not to trim hedges, work in a fast-food joint, or empty other people's trash cans.

So I make a number of these cardboard signs, all with slight variations. I have one that reads:

PLEASE HELP. GIRLFRIEND LEFT ME FOR ANOTHER MAN. NOW ARMS HOLD NO ONE, HEART BROKEN. DEPRESSED. ANY SMALL CHANGE WILL DO.

The only issue with the different signs is that I have to use them at different locations, far removed from each other. Obviously, the same people frequent the same subway station so I can't take a chance that someone will see two different messages. I'd be exposed for sure.

* * *

My favourite way to make a bit of extra money is to dispense advice. Short clever sayings that I've lifted from famous philosophers. I ask $1 in exchange. I have them all on little scraps of paper that I keep in a bowler hat; people reach in and pick one and usually start laughing. I often get more than the asked-for $1. I never reveal who actually wrote the sayings though … I figure I'll get more money if people think I had written them. But they're all little ditties about life and love:

> *"Happiness is the meaning and the purpose of life, the whole aim and end of human existence."*
> — *Aristotle.*

> *"Happiness is like a butterfly; the more you chase it, the more it will elude you, but if you turn your attention to other things, it will come and sit softly on your shoulder."*
> — *Henry David Thoreau.*

> *"Life isn't about finding yourself. Life is about creating yourself."*
> — *George Bernard Shaw.*

> *"Why should we build our happiness on the opinions of others, when we can find it in our own hearts?"*
> — *Jean-Jacques Rousseau.*

I simply remove the quotation marks and the name of the person who penned the words. And I have a lot of uplifting quotes about happiness. I think most people want to know about that. In fact, the sign on my piece of cardboard reads:

THE HAPPINESS GURU.
$1 FOR A SLICE OF HAPPINESS.

Brilliant.

***

When I wasn't begging for money, I usually wandered around the city. I had all this free time and needed something to do. I didn't wander aimlessly, rather I considered myself an explorer of sorts, investigating hidden areas. And often I ventured out in the late evenings. I found solace with a group of vagrants who lived under the Bloor Street Viaduct. I felt alright in their company, they didn't ask questions. Not even my name. I regaled them with stories of my years in the philosophy department at the University of Toronto, where I had punched out my academic advisor when he slandered me. Swinging uppercut, then a straight jab.

"Like this," I shouted, throwing an uppercut. "And like that. Take that." Another swing.

I also told them about my idea that I was a Superman, modelled after Nietzsche's work. "I'm an *Ubermensch*," I said to a phalanx of shaking heads.

"Ubermankle!" they shouted in unison, drunkenly fumbling with the word and lifting their wine bottles to me.

Hiding in the ravine by day, my new friends ventured out only at night, usually to collect beer bottles or else forage for food. They all had their own tales of woe but now treated each other like family, sharing food and drink.

There was no point in sleeping under the bridge since I still had my own apartment. At least for now. But I visited the ravine dwellers as often as I could, that is, whenever my mood allowed. Some nights though I couldn't get out of bed at all; there seemed to be no point. Aside from the ravine, I had nowhere to go. But there were benefits to not getting up. I found that when I lay in bed all day, I didn't have much of an appetite. That saved on food bills.

***

On one occasion, I discovered a whole forbidden city of homeless and derelict people, living in tents and makeshift shelters and eating by campfire. It was called Tent Haven and was located down by the waterfront. I wandered in as if I belonged and no one said a word. Dozens of empty cough syrup bottles were strewn on the ground, as were an assortment of needles. Orange flames emanated from steel barrels, as far as the eye could see. I wondered how it was that the cops hadn't shut the place down. Surely they must have known. Maybe on the list of insidious crimes that derailed Toronto, those being committed at Tent Haven were pretty low.

Carnival City, that's what I called the place. I returned each night and quickly found out that most everyone had a lunar mind that veered off into indecipherable conversations. Many were stoned or drunk. Some mentally unstable, like Edna. When I first met her, she ran her hands down her body in quick jerky motions, as if trying to brush off imaginary insects.

"Do you know who I am?" she asked.

"No."

"Let me tell you something. I used to be somebody."

She jabbed her forefinger into my chest for emphasis. "SOMEBODY. GOT IT?"

"Yes, I understand," I said in a mollifying voice. Almost at once, I could tell what sort of person I was dealing with.

"Then I started collecting things. I couldn't throw anything away. Bottles, bottle caps, bits of paper, used paper cups, old magazines and newspapers, pencils, half-eaten bagels, empty pill bottles, broken toys, cracked planters, used books, movie ticket stubs, receipts, clothes that I had outgrown, shoes with the heels worn down, rusty pots and pans, socks with holes in them, blankets with holes in them, hair that came out in the sink, lint from the dryer, crooked nails, straight nails, pieces of cotton, candy wrappers, empty shampoo bottles, empty cereal boxes, empty detergent boxes, old food cartons, dead bugs, used dental floss ... anyway, there's a lot more but you get the idea. I couldn't move in my own apartment. There was no place to eat. I used to eat standing up. Nobody ever came over, I wouldn't let anyone. I didn't want them to think I was crazy."

"You were a hoarder?"

"No, just a collector."

"Anyway, why are you telling me this?"

"Because you think I might have brain damage, that's why."

"I don't think that."

"Don't flatter me. You're such a liar."

I should have walked away but didn't. As disgusted as I felt about a homeless woman who was wearing a tattered pink terry cloth bathrobe and with her hair in curlers, I also felt sorry for Edna. Maybe she had been a somebody at one time, although I doubted it. But now she was just pathetic, a shrivelled-up shrew. There was something else: I was ... well ... lonely, and wanted to talk to someone. Especially to someone who wasn't drunk all the time like my friends under the bridge. I didn't smell any liquor on Edna's breath.

"Maybe I wasn't too well then but now it's different," she said. "I'm alright now. But I'll tell you, it was a long road. A psychiatrist from the Department of Health came over to the apartment, the first person ever. I think the landlord sent him. So this guy brought some boxes and said he wanted me to organize things. *Organize,* just imagine! I knew what he was up to. That organizing was nothing more than preparing me to get rid of my stuff."

"Why did you keep all that junk anyway?" I asked.

"Excuse me, but it wasn't *junk*, as you call it. Everything I kept was special. Had its own special texture. Everything felt unique to the touch. Some things smooth, others rough. Some things round, others square. Some things paper, others metal. Every time I touched something, it felt like I had almost ... hmmm ... anointed it. Made it sacred, you know. Can't explain it better."

"Anointed?"

"Yes. What of it?"

"Who did you think you were? Jesus Christ?" As soon as the words slipped out, I knew it was a mistake.

"You are one pig of a man. You think you're better than me, don't you?"

"Maybe I am." Again, a wrong choice.

Edna stared at me without saying a word. One eyebrow arched high, her mug screwed up tight as a drum, hard and frank.

"You're a piss poor excuse for a human being," she said.

I didn't need that. I started walking away, but Edna ran after me in her high-heeled shoes, almost stumbling on the stubbly, rock-hard ground. One shoe fell off.

'Wait, don't you want to know what happened with the psychiatrist?"

If there was one thing I came to realize about the people at Tent Haven, it was that they may have been down-and-outers, but they were for the most part harmless. I stopped and listened; the story at least, was mildly entertaining.

"Well, so he came in with these boxes labelled Hard, Medium and Easy," Edna said quietly, seemingly more at ease now that she had an audience again. "Hard to throw away, easy to throw away, and things that were in the middle, not hard, not easy—medium. When we started, I put everything into the Hard boxes. He then tried to convince me that some things in those boxes, a few things, could be moved into the Medium boxes, things like hair, bugs, lint. But I couldn't bear to part with anything. This guy just didn't get it. When I was about to put something in the Hard box, he would grab hold of my hand and move it to the Medium box, trying to get me to drop it there. I thought he was crazy, a mad fool. Why did he think that my own hair meant nothing to me? And bugs are so interesting to touch, they're not like anything else."

I furrowed my brow but remained silent. Why was I wasting my time with this lunatic?

"Don't make faces like that."

"Sorry."

"Good, so now let me finish. As I was saying … hmmm …" Edna paused for a moment and looked at her feet. "Missing one shoe," she said remorsefully. "And now I forgot what I was saying."

"You were talking about the Hard, Medium and Easy boxes. How the psychiatrist tried to make you move things from the Hard box to the Medium box."

"Ah … yeah, yeah, you're right," she said, suddenly remembering. "By the way, do you have a cigarette?"

I pulled out my pack of Gitanes and gave Edna one.

"Can I have another?"

"Sure."

Edna took a long drag, and blew a tight spiral into the air. "So there I was and this shrink guy—I forget his name—was holding my hand over the Medium box, shaking it, forcing me to let go of whatever I was holding. He was much stronger than me so he was able to make me drop things. He was a brute. That was his idea of getting me to learn to *organize*. But every time things went into the Medium box, I started crying. It was so hard, I can't tell you." Edna started mumbling under her breath. "So, what was I telling you?"

"You were describing how the psychiatrist forced you to put things in the Medium box."

"The Medium box. Now I remember. Anyway, every night when the guy left, I would take things from the Medium box and put them back in the Hard box. So in the morning when he came back, there was hardly anything left in the Medium box."

A spasm rocked Edna's right hand.

"You ok?"

Edna laughed nervously. "I got a touch of Parkinson's. Body's out of control. Does what it wants. Strange how things work out."

"What's strange?"

"I always used to do want *I* wanted. My brain had its own desires which I always followed. We were buds. Now my body is doing what *it* wants. Except I can't follow it like I did my brain. It's like it's separate from me. Get my drift?"

"I get your drift." I didn't, but it made no difference.

Edna picked up with her story. "So this shrink guy got really upset with me. Said my only hope was to get electroshock treatments down at the hospital where he worked. There was something in my brain that needed to be zapped with electricity. They'd done work like that with criminals and depressed people. People who just couldn't get it together. He assured me I wouldn't feel a thing; they'd give me lots of drugs. Sedating stuff."

"Did you go?"

"No, I didn't want them to zap me. I was a somebody, you know, just like I told you. I didn't want them messing with that. Then I'd be a nobody. So I thought that, if I could find a job, he'd get off my case. The only reason he got interested in me at all was because I was collecting disability insurance from the province. Couldn't work because of my habit of collecting things."

"So you went to look for a job?"

"Yeah. I went down to the local employment agency. They asked me what skills I had—did I have computer skills, how fast could I type … stuff like that. Well, I couldn't do any of that. But I did know how to save things. I was pretty good at it. They didn't really understand but it didn't matter. I found the perfect job—filing in the office for an activist organization that was hellbent on saving the redwood trees."

Edna was rambling. The story was going nowhere and I was getting tired.

"I think I have to go now," I said.

Edna grabbed hold of my arm with her reed-like fingers. "Don't go. The rest of the story's pretty interesting."

"Make it quick."

"Ok, so there I was, working in the office. I got started in the filing room but the problem of saving things started all over again. I couldn't throw anything away. The filing room got quite messy. Became like my apartment. You couldn't move and I couldn't file anything anymore. I also couldn't find anything."

"Did they fire you?"

"Nah. Some of the leaders in the group decided that, since they liked my commitment, they would just find me a more suitable position."

"Where?"

"I couldn't really work in the office, anywhere indoors actually, that's where I ran into trouble. That's when we came up with the idea of working outside, with the trees."

"You planted trees?"

"No, better than that. I lived in a tree. Up a redwood. About one-hundred-and-twenty-feet up. Lived there for a year."

"You lived up in a redwood tree for a year? Like fuck you did."

"Sonny, I sure did. Just to stop them trees getting cut down by loggers."

I was full of wonderment that anyone could concoct such a story so I stayed on to listen and see what other crazy stuff would spill forth from the woman's mouth.

"We need them trees," Edna said. "For the animals, birds and plants. Salmon lay their eggs in the forest streams. Just imagine if all the redwoods were gone? What would happen to all the black bears and foxes? What about beautiful plants like rhododendrons and wood sorrels? Seems to me you wouldn't see none of them woodpeckers either. Not only that but there'd be a lot more earth slides without the trees to hold the soil in place."

Edna took another drag of her cigarette and exhaled deeply. "And it's not just in the forests where we need more trees—it's in the cities too. If you walk down a main street in any big city you'll see those skimpy decorative trees growing out of planter tubs. A long time ago, cities had lots of large trees lining the downtown core. Elms, sugar maples, oak. Beautiful canopies. They're good for cleaning the air and they cut down on noise levels. The problem is that when cities start to grow, things like sewers and buried cables and that there begin to take up space underground. Them tree roots gets all constricted. And then above ground, you've got telephone and hydro lines."

The more I listened to Edna, the more I began to think that she knew an awful lot about what she was saying. Maybe I had misjudged her. Maybe there was a modicum of truth in what she was saying. Still, it seemed preposterous, the whole business of living up in a redwood. Maybe she was just repeating something she had read in a book. A child's story about living in a tree, a book of fiction that lodged in her disturbed brain. I just couldn't tell.

"Didn't the loggers try to get you down?" I asked.

"Yeah, you bet. They sent people up a few times. Didn't come all the way up but close enough to insult me and threaten me with lawsuits. They used floodlights and loud sirens. Once they had a helicopter fly over the tree. That wasn't the worst part though."

"Not the worst part?"

"No, the worst part were them rainstorms. I had to hold on to the tree for my dear life. The funny part was that I always felt I'd be ok because I knew the tree would take care of me. I really developed a relationship with that tree. Called her Maggie. She knew I was there to protect her and so she did the same for me."

"So if all that was true, why did you come down?" I said. "And by the way, how did you get your food?

"So I'll answer the last question first. One of them guys in the office, he was an engineer. He made this pulley system, so everything came up and down on a small wooden platform, like this." Edna pulled on imaginary ropes. "Now as to why I came down … well, that's another story. I guess you can say that I made my point. The logging company would've got a lot of bad press if they had a cut Maggie down, especially after all the media attention. The other thing was that I was getting kind of tired up there. I had this bad chest cough that wouldn't go away and my lower back was sore a lot from sleeping on a thin mattress. It was just time. I gave Maggie one last hug, a big kiss, and came down on the platform."

It was like that there down by the lake. Everybody had a story, made up or not. It was just up to you whether you wanted to believe it. But I was a philosopher and realized that anything logical was possible. The universe was infinite as far as I was concerned and that meant there was an infinite number of possibilities, including Edna's redwood tree story. Perhaps she had in fact turned a possibility into reality. I would never know.

All I knew with certainty is that Edna seemed to be vibrating. Perhaps it was the Parkinson's. But her entire body seemed to be pulsing with what seemed like emotion. Tears filled her eyes. She looked at me with her wide-open, teary eyes, like she was expecting me to say something. But there really was nothing to say. And even if I found flaws in her story, if I found it completely implausible, who was I to deny her?

EASY COME, EASY GO

When my mom was alive, she arranged for me to meet a woman. This was a first since I had no experience with women. I hadn't been on a date in my life. In high school, I didn't go to the school prom and had never once been to any party. And in high school, there were many. Aside from the fact that no one ever asked me, I never had any interest. The parties were mostly for the "cool kids" and that was definitely not me. In fact, sometimes my classmates would walk past me in the hallway or outside of school and pretend not to know me ... they would avert their eyes or look down at the ground. But when I got older, about eighteen or so, my mom thought it might be a good idea for me to meet someone. A girl. There was a problem though—I didn't know what I would do with one. What was the point? I had no experience with relationships. That didn't deter my mom though. She was determined to set me up with someone.

"I refuse to do this," I said.

"You have no choice," my mom said. "Now be on your best behaviour please."

***

For a time, especially after my father died, my mother became quite social and seemed to know a lot of people. Even prospective women for me.

Zsofia Rosenblatt was the first girl to show up. She came with her parents and we all sat around in the living room and had chamomile tea, my hot drink of choice, and cookies my mom put out. Zsofia had dirty blonde hair cut in a short bob and her brown eyebrows met together in the middle so they looked like a crow in flight. She looked to be a few years older than me. Maybe more than a few, early or mid-twenties I guessed. I wore a white shirt and a blue tie my mom helped me with. I crossed my legs and swung them back and forth. The strangers, Mr. Rosenblatt wearing a white skullcap and Mrs. Rosenblatt sporting a very stiff red wig that looked like it was formed out of plaster, made me nervous. That was not a good sign since they had only just arrived. They were Jewish quite obviously and I had never known anyone Jewish before. It was a first for me. It was surprising to me that my mom knew any Jews either. She was Roma from Hungary, and it just seemed that Roma and Jews travelled in different circles. But like I said, she started meeting more and more people after my father passed. And what did I know, really? I was still very young.

"I love music," Mrs. Rosenblatt said to my mom, munching on a chocolate chip cookie. "Klezmer a little bit but mostly prayer songs sung by a chazzan in a synagogue. Whenever I hear it, I am taken away to lovely places."

"Yes," Mr. Rosenblatt said. "Lovely places. The Wailing Wall in Jerusalem." He clapped his hands together. "Jerusalem was destroyed and rebuilt nine times, do you know, and only one symbol stayed up all the time."

"The Western Wall," Mrs. Rosenblatt said, closing her eyes as if secretly praying before it.

Zsofia, who was sitting with her parents on the sofa, turned to me. "What do you think of music?"

"Not much," I said abruptly. "But my mom loves Paul McCartney. When she cooks, she sings his songs. I think she thinks she's the female version of McCartney."

I couldn't tell what the Rosenblatts thought of my remark. They seemed to mumble 'oh my' in unison. But what I could tell for sure was that my mom wasn't happy with it. She sucked in her lips and explained rather quickly that, while she loved McCartney's music, she was a rank amateur compared to him.

Mr. Rosenblatt told us he worked in a fish market and sometimes brought home fish bones for an amazing fish broth that his wife prepared for Sabbath evenings.

"Yes, I use a slow cooker and let the bones simmer with vegetables—onions, carrots, turnips, celery, tomatoes, garlic," Mrs. Rosenblatt said. "I use bay leaves, sea salt, parsley, cloves, peppercorn. I cook up some yellow rice to put in the broth when it's done. A little horseradish to finish. It's a recipe my mother, God rest her soul, brought back from the old country when she arrived. Minsk, in Belarus."

"Technically, tomatoes are a fruit," I said.

"What do you mean?" Mrs. Rosenblatt asked.

"You said tomatoes are a vegetable. They're really a fruit."

My mom pointed her forefinger at me and shook it, like she was shaking off some blood.

"Vegetable ... fruit," Mr. Rosenblatt said. "It doesn't matter. It's delicious. The next time, we will bring you and Karl here a big bowl of the fish broth."

"Noooooo!" I wasn't about to eat fish broth. No way.

My mom covered her face with her hands and very quickly turned her attention to the Rosenblatts' daughter.

"So Zsofia, are you in school? Working?"

"Both actually. I'm working for an accounting firm and studying for my CPA at night."

"Excuse my ignorance but I don't know what a CPA is," my mom said.

"Chartered Professional Accountant," Zsofia said.

"Maybe you should study nutrition," I said suddenly. "Good nutrition is the foundation for a healthy life."

I looked at Zsofia, who had put down her oatmeal cookie. Her face had scrunched up considerably, like she had swallowed a lemon or something. Her face was as very round and big as the moon. It was pudgy all over, which wasn't too surprising since she was, in my opinion, about thirty pounds overweight.

"Excuse me," she said, putting great emphasis on the words.

"What's your BMI anyway?" I asked her.

She didn't know what that meant. Neither did the Rosenblatts. It appeared my mom may have known though because she cupped her knees with the palms of her hands and began rocking back and forth in her chair.

"Karl, that's not important," she said. "Why don't you tell our guests about your ambition. It's an interesting one."

So I explained that I hoped to become a philosophy professor one day.

"That's admirable," Zsofia said. "A solid job. Does that mean you hope to have a family one day?"

That didn't make any sense to me at all. What did wanting to be a professor have to do with children? I immediately sensed that Zsofia was a complete dunderhead.

"No. I don't like children," I said. "They're annoying."

I wasn't sure what happened but Mr. Rosenblatt stood up to leave, followed by Mrs. Rosenblatt and Zsofia. We were in the middle of an interesting conversation about fish broth and the Wailing Wall and BMIs and my desire to excel at school and get a job and they just decided to cut it all short. I stayed sitting, my legs still swinging madly, but my mom followed the family out the front door. I overheard her saying "I'm so sorry, I'm so sorry." I didn't understand why she was apologizing. What I did know now was why the Rosenblatts were trying to set their daughter up. Good luck to them, they would need it.

* * *

My mom didn't give up after that, although she probably should have. "From now on," she said, "you're going to visit the women I'm setting you up with. They're not coming to our apartment because you're too comfortable there and that makes you say whatever you want. You will go to the woman's place and be on your best behaviour. Bring flowers. Or a box of designer cookies. I'll help you pick something out. One way or the other, I am going to set you up with a nice woman."

"It's not a good idea," I said. "And once again I refuse."

"You will go and you will be on your best behaviour. You will show interest in the women and compliment them. And if you don't, you will not be allowed back in my home."

I wanted to cry. My mom sounded very, very serious. More serious than ever. And where would I go if I weren't allowed back home?

* * *

Two more attempts at setting me up failed just as miserably as the first. There's no point in talking about them, I'd rather forget. I just didn't have very good social skills. But I know they disturbed my mom, and that was the worst part. I hated disappointing her. Much to her credit though, she didn't give up. She was really resilient.

"One more try," she told me. "You need this."

So her next attempt to set me up with a woman was with Erica. Mom told me she had never met her before and didn't even know her parents.

"She's pretty," she said. "I've seen a picture."

"How do you know her then?"

"That's my business."

"It's my business too if I'm going to meet her."

"Look, give her a chance, Karl. And bring some designer cookies and Fair Trade coffee. That's a nice start. And drink the coffee. No chamomile tea either. Come, let's go shopping."

* * *

"What did you bring?" Erica said, rummaging through the plastic bag I was carrying. "Let me see here. Coffee, cream, cookies. Perfect. I'll start the coffee." She gave

136

me a wink, a conspiratorial wink so it seemed, and headed to the kitchen.

I sat down on a white leather sofa in the spacious living room. The smell of marijuana permeated the air; I recognized it from school, where many students indulged on the grounds. I looked around the room: It was at least three times the size of my mom's living room. Huge. With a fireplace that crackled wood and a wall-mounted TV that must have been at least sixty-four inches. I had never been in an apartment like this before. Especially one that was on the thirty-second floor of a high-rise building. My mom's building only had six floors and had no concierge in the lobby.

I took a Kleenex from my pocket and plugged my nose with tiny pieces; unlike years later when I started smoking in earnest, I just couldn't stand the smell of the dope. But it was crazy that I was here. I felt terribly out of place and my legs were swinging madly. I suspected that my arms might soon follow. A flailing marionette.

"Where is your mom?" I called out. I was trying to be social, like my mom wanted me to be.

Erica stuck her head around a wall that separated the kitchen from the living room. "She had to go out," she said, laughing. "Very suddenly."

"Where did she go?" I said, not understanding what was so funny about the question.

"Dunno."

"When is she coming back?"

"Didn't say."

"I guess you can't rely on her too much. Not like my mom."

Erica returned with a tray holding two mugs of steaming coffee, the cream, and a bowl of brown sugar.

There were no cookies in sight although I noticed some cookie crumbs on her lips. I guessed that was ok. I didn't really have a sweet tooth anyway, so if she ate all the cookies, that was just fine with me.

I looked carefully at Erica. She was very tall, pretty, with hazel eyes, long black hair with grey highlights, and full, pouty lips. It didn't matter to me though, although I supposed that if I were ever to have a relationship with a woman, she might as well have been pretty. *Relationship with a woman?* That was not on my agenda. Not at all. Still, I wondered how my mom knew Erica, But then, she sometimes came off as a woman of mystery … I never did find out how she even knew the Rosenblatts.

"I've never had a girlfriend before," I suddenly blurted out.

"Well, that's just fine with me. I'm not looking for a boyfriend." Erica put down her coffee cup and moved closer on the sofa. She crossed her legs and her short black skirt ran up to her thighs. She then put her hand on my shoulder and it sent a strange chill through my body, almost like an electric volt.

"There's plenty of space at the other end of the sofa," I said. "Plus I don't like anyone touching me."

Erica smiled knowingly. "Peachy," she said, sipping her coffee. "We can talk. We can talk for a while. So, how's work for you? You work in a bank, right?"

"What?"

"Not a bank? Ok, I just guessed based on your personality. So why don't you tell me what you do."

I waved Erica away. "Go sit over there." I pointed to the far end of the sofa. Unfortunately, Erica wouldn't budge. She was sitting inches away. I considered gently pushing her but suspected my mom wouldn't like that.

I slid over to the far end of my side of the sofa, as far as I could, which wasn't very far indeed. The fingers on Erica's left hand started walking bizarrely over to me, like a spider crawling on eight legs, or in this case, five fingers. What exactly was this silly person up to?

"I should have been born a vampire," she said. "You see?" She showed me her teeth. Her incisors looked a bit pointy, but not any more so than anyone else's from what I could determine. Certainly not like Dracula's teeth.

"What?"

And that was it. Erica climbed on top of me and started nibbling my neck. I jumped up and screamed but she pulled me back down and started biting once more. She asked me if I liked *sense*. I didn't know what she meant and told her as much. So she showed me, moving her neck close to my nose and telling me to have a whiff.

"Take that silly Kleenex out of your nostrils," she said.

Oh, ok, so now I got it—*scents*. I removed the wads of Kleenex and gossamers of perfume wafted to my nose. I could feel myself swooning, dropping deep into a black void. I thought I would faint. So I was utterly helpless when Erica kissed me passionately on the lips. I should have protested, told her that this was all wrong, shoved her away, something, but I couldn't ... I was her prisoner, there was no escaping. It was the first time in my life that anything like this had ever happened and I had no idea how to react. But there I was, not exactly kissing this strange woman back, but not resisting either.

She was wearing all black—a black top, black skirt, black leggings. With copious amounts of black mascara and her long black hair (dyed with streaks of grey as I said), she resembled Morticia from *The Addams Family*, a TV show I had sometimes watched. Maybe that was it. I always found Morticia alluring in a weird way. Like I wanted to have a picnic with her in a cemetery, surrounded by lit candelabras.

My heart was thumping and my penis, a part I had never used before other than for peeing, began vibrating. I wasn't sure what came next but Erica seemed to know exactly what to do. She stood up and led me by the hand to the bedroom. My shoe splashed in a pan of aquamarine coloured paint. This was bad, very, very bad indeed.

"Oh no," I said. "My mom will kill me. She recently bought me these running shoes."

"Yah well, my bedroom is being painted and the painter left his paint. Not a big deal but sorry anyway."

Something, I wasn't exactly sure what, but suspected they were what people called 'hormones,' were raging and I kicked off the wet shoe. Then the other. We flopped onto the bed and as we were rolling around, I wanted to get up and leave before something really bad happened. I tried twice but couldn't; every time I made a move to stand up, Erica pulled me back down. After the second attempt, I no longer resisted. Oh my word, what was happening to me? My head was swooning, I couldn't think properly, and my body was acting of its own accord.

"You can't avoid fate," she said.

I had no idea what she was talking about but it didn't matter, I just wanted this to continue.

My mouth was drooling like some mad animal and I started sucking and kissing every inch of Erica's body.

Very suddenly, she pushed me away and reached for something in a night table.

"Here, put this on," she said, thrusting the box at me. "Hurry."

I looked at the box. "No idea what this is," I said.

"Oh for heaven's sake." Erica reached into the box and took out a piece of plastic which she ripped open. She expertly placed the plastic over my erect penis.

Then we were fucking. I screamed. My glasses fell off.

It was over very quickly. Erica pulled a cigarette from a pack on the night table and took a long drag. She offered but I declined. I was exhausted, sweaty, and my right sock was soaking wet with paint. I lay on my back and tried to breathe deeply but couldn't. I was incredibly nervous and my arms started flapping uncontrollably. Like I was possessed or something.

"After effects," Erica said.

"I have no idea what you mean."

Erica blew a perfect ring of smoke; it lingered for a few seconds and then dissipated into the ether. Dissolving margins.

I stood up in a hurry and put my clothes on. "I have to go," I said. "I'm from the Pleiades and need to get back. It's a long journey."

"Where is that?"

I explained to Erica that it was another planetary system, many light years away. I had often told my classmates when I was growing up that I was from there. Just to compensate for being different.

"You're weird."

"I'm glad you think so."

"Silly boy. You know you can't avoid fate."

"Why do you keep saying that?" I asked.

"That's the name of my perfume."

I should have figured that one out. But I still wasn't thinking clearly. I felt unsteady and started whimpering.

"What the ...?" Erica said, perplexed.

"It's just that no one has touched me ... ever. So I'm kind of emotional."

"Too bad. And take your cookies with you, they'll make me fat. And ..."

"Yes?"

"Tell your mother she owes me."

* * *

I was glad my mom wasn't home. I took a hot shower and washed myself all over with soap. When I thought I was clean, I started all over again. Then I lay in my bed and curled up under a mountain of blankets. I started crying and didn't think I would ever stop. I just kept repeating the word "why" in my head over and over again. Why would my mom set me up with a girl like Erica? I didn't get it, although I guess she had her reasons.

* * *

Many years later, when my mom had passed and I was living alone, I often dreamt about women. Needless to say, they were always erotic dreams. But quite frankly, there were times I got tired of satisfying myself. So on the few occasions when I had a bit of money, I splurged on a real woman. I knew exactly what I wanted—blonde, slim, about five-feet, seven inches or so, lily-white and busty. I checked online for escort agencies in Toronto and was overwhelmed by the choices. A smorgasbord of human flesh. Every conceivable yearning could be satisfied for a price. I had no desire to be whipped or spanked or to grovel but thought it might be fun to have someone in a nurse's outfit cater to me. Pretend to take my temperature and start me off with warm compresses. That is, until I realized that really, I only cared about one thing.

I finally settled on an agency called Come Girl. They catered to "discriminating gentlemen" and that was fine by me. They also had in their fold a wide variety of women from different regions of the world—Russia, China, Japan, the Middle East, Scandinavia, the U.S; curiously though, none from Canada. Perhaps Canadians were simply not in high demand. Just too familiar perhaps, I had no idea. It wasn't of any importance though as I scanned through the agency's girls online and quickly settled on a statuesque blonde from Sweden. *Ingrid*, what else?

I phoned the agency and told them that I preferred if Ingrid came to my place, which was fine, except they needed to meet with me first. "Too many weirdos out there," I was told.

I showered and shaved and put on my best sweater, my only one in fact. I then bought a 13-dollar bottle of white wine and made my way to Come Girl. It was on the third floor of an industrial warehouse in the west end of the city and the sign on the front door said "Orion Casting and Modelling." I met with Mrs. Kelly, the proprietor, a rather skinny, unattractive woman with an unruly mane of jet-black hair.

"You look like Russ Meyer," she said.

"I don't know Russ Meyer."

"He made pornographic movies in the 1970s. He had a thing for large-breasted women."

"Is that bad?"

"No, I'm just saying."

I removed the wine from a brown paper bag. "Here, this is for you."

"I don't drink but I'm sure one of the girls will enjoy it. Thank you."

I explained that I was a PhD student in philosophy and lonely for female company. My schedule was gruelling, non-stop what with helping to tutor undergraduates, writing my thesis, attending lectures.

"You look a little old to be a full-time student."

Again with the looks. I simply shrugged my shoulders.

"I have two questions for you," Mrs. Kelly said. "First, do you have a record? And, do you like to hurt women?"

"No and no."

"We can't be too careful. The girls that work for me are my employees and I have to look out for their well-being."

"I understand completely," I said. "Don't worry, I'm completely harmless."

"Good." At that point, Mrs. Kelly explained how business worked. Condoms were a must. Ingrid could stay the night but there was an extra $50. I had to pay her cab fare back to the office and that cost $25. No pals were to be hiding in closets when Ingrid got to the apartment; that is, no threesomes, no orgies. No anal sex. No drugs. Money had to be paid up front. Cash only. Those were the rules. Everything else was negotiable.

I left Come Girl with a list of written prices. It was a little like a restaurant menu except that all the food was human flesh. And because I was a full-time student, I was able to show my University of Toronto library card, and get a twenty percent discount.

* * *

Ingrid showed up at my front door, looking exactly as her picture. Stunning. There were no surprises. No drugs, no weed, nothing, I remembered that, but Mrs. Kelly never said anything about wine. So we each had a glass of Chardonnay. Then it was straight to bed. I couldn't hold off any longer.

There was no foreplay, as Ingrid had suggested. A little nibbling, a little kissing, a little holding—all of it was out of the question. It was my money, I told her, so my rules. Besides, I just wanted *in* very badly. Ingrid left that night, I had no desire to spend another $50. I felt fabulous, why spoil things?

When the money allowed, I saw Ingrid. We rarely spoke, it was all about the sex. Silence and sex, it was the perfect relationship.

THE LOVER

I've had exactly one serious relationship in my life and I owe it all to literature. To my desire to write prose. Fiction. And it all harkens back to high school, when I first became interested in books. Not comic books or science texts, which were my mainstays of reading. But real literature. And as unlikely as it was, I owe it all to my mom. She had been a reader much of her life, especially when she came to Toronto from Hungary and learned English really well. So one day she gave me a book called *Great Expectations*, by someone called Charles Dickens. It was a great big tome of a book and I railed against reading it, saying I didn't have the time, that I was just about to start reading a giant comic book called *Legends of Tomorrow*. It cost me $7.99, which was a fortune for a comic book, and I told my mom as much.

"I gave you that money," she replied.

"It's an anthology," I said, ignoring her last remark. "Firestorm is the most popular character and his matrix is malfunctioning. That's a problem. Then there's Metamorpho; well really he's the archaeologist Rex Mason but he turned into Metamorpho after he touched the Orb of Ra."

I was going to tell her about the remaining characters, Sugar and Spike, and Metal Men, but she snatched the comic book from my night table, where all my comic books were piled up in stacks, and put it in a cardboard box. Then she rounded up the rest of the comic books, which numbered in the hundreds, and put them in the box as well.

"Here, read," she said, plopping *Great Expectations* on my bed.

So there I was, without any of my beloved comics, and after my mom left my room, tears welled up in my eyes. How could she do that to me? I thought we were a team. I thought she was looking out for me. Now I wasn't so sure. All I knew was that I didn't want to read this Charles Dickens guy. Why would he write such a big book in the first place? Didn't he have anything better to do with his time?

I decided I had better Google Dickens. I knew my mom would expect me to read his book. She was like that; when she said something, I knew she meant business. So I thought that, before I even opened the book up, it would be best to find something out about the author. There might even have been an abridged version of *Great Expectations* online.

The first thing I noticed was that Dickens had a very long pointy beard, all straggly. It looked strange, as if something horrible and dirty was growing in it. And his hair appeared windswept, terribly messy, like he had never used a comb on it. Now for sure I didn't feel like reading his work—if he couldn't take care of himself, chances were that his novel wasn't very good.

I carried on though. There was simply no choice. So it seemed that Dickens left school to work in a blacking factory when his father was incarcerated in a debtors' prison. That's what the 'net said. I couldn't figure any of that out—I had no idea what a blacking factory or debtors' prison was. He left school early and was uneducated, that's all I got. It was all I needed, I walked out of my bedroom and confronted my mom, who was busy in the living room practising singing.

"Can I have my comic books back, please?" I made sure to say *please*. Her voice was hitting some very high notes so I had to make sure my own voice was very loud.

My mom stopped singing.

"What's that again? I only caught a part of what you said."

"I said, can I have my comic books back please."

"Have you started reading *Great Expectations*?"

"No."

"Then no."

Back in my room, I decided I would talk the next day to my high school English teacher, Mr. Sylvestre. He seemed nice enough, never calling on me in class to answer questions, like some of the other teachers. He was very tall and skinny. And his clothes were always very neat and tidy; he never wore jeans like some other teachers but rather nicely pressed pants. He always had on a jacket and a bow tie. He told us he was from England.

* * *

"What's your interest in Charles Dickens?"

It was a simple enough question but I wasn't sure how to answer Mr. Sylvestre. I didn't exactly want to tell him that my mom had taken away all my comic books and was forcing me to read *Great Expectations*. He didn't have to know about my interest in comic books. It was bad enough that he didn't think much of my home planet in the Pleiades. When growing up, I had often told my classmates that that was where I was from and the teachers found out. Anyway, I knew that he wasn't a fan because he once told me to cut it out, to stop pretending to be from another planet, that I was *bigger than that*. That was the one and only time he had spoken to me and I wasn't even sure what he meant by saying "I was bigger than that." I didn't actually mind when he said all that though, it was only his opinion. Like I said, as long as he didn't ask me questions in class, I was on good terms with him.

"I was given *Great Expectations* as a gift," I said. That was true enough.

"Well, in my opinion, Dickens was the greatest novelist of all time. Oh, I'll get plenty of people who will beg to differ, who will say it was someone else, maybe Dostoyevsky or Tolstoy or another writer. Yet others might say John Irving. Ha! Why, some people even say Stephen King is the greatest novelist! But no other fiction writer has created so many characters that people still know today. Think about it—Oliver Twist, The Artful Dodger, Fagin, Scrooge, Tiny Tim, Little Dorrit, David Copperfield, Mr. Micawber, Uriah Heep, Pip, Mr. Gradgrind ... good Lord, the list goes on and on."

Mr. Sylvestre took a deep breath. "Dickens showed the underbelly of Victorian England in his novels. You know what that means, do you, Karl, the *underbelly*?

"No, Mr. Sylvestre, I don't know what that means."

"It means the seamy side. The dark side."

"I see." I still wasn't sure what exactly that all meant but I didn't want to say as much. I didn't want Mr. Sylvestre to think I wasn't smart.

"Of course, although we see a lot of dark characters who embody the hypocrisy of British class, in Dickens we also see goodness of heart, and wonderful outcomes."

Mr. Sylvestre closed his eyes and started nodding his head, like he was in the middle of a very private dream. It was then that I noticed a lot of dark hairs coming out of his nose, something I had never noticed before. I decided I should cut off the conversation right then.

"Thanks, Mr. Sylvestre. I have to go."

"Wait." Mr. Sylvestre grabbed me by the arm. As a rule, I didn't like people touching me, but in this case, there seemed no way out. "Just one more thing, young man."

"Ok, then I have to go."

"Read *Great Expectations*. It will change your life."

***

I guess Mr. Sylvestre was right. Because after I read through *Great Expectations* in its entirety and Googled information about the author, I felt I had just emerged from a dream. One in which I had been in Victorian England. But it was dirty and overcrowded and ugly in London, and the cattle market, where people could buy sheep and cattle, with its blood and filth and fat, made me sick, so I was happy to stop daydreaming and return to Toronto.

***

So that was the start, when I realized that literature could transport me to other places. Places full of wonderment and delight. That's what I got from books. Of course my first love was philosophy but I dreamt of being a best-selling author. And when you're an unemployed philosopher, as I was for a great deal of my life, you have a lot of time to try your hand at writing. So I did. Not that I had any talent, I knew that. But at least I could try.

One day then I set up shop at a coffee shop on Eglinton Avenue, ordered a coffee and a bran muffin, and set out to write. A novella. That was the way to go, I figured. Write something short, where I could envision an ending. Novels were too long and winding, with many back-stories and endings I couldn't foresee. And actually, I had been reading a strange novel called *The Golems of Gotham* by Thane Rosenbaum and thought I would try my hand at something esoteric like that.

But almost as soon as I started, I noticed a woman staring at me. She was quite pretty, with sumptuous plump lips, a light-café-aux-lait complexion, and a smattering of childlike freckles dotting her aquiline nose. Her braided light brown hair was piled impressively high on her head, seemingly defying the laws of ordinary gravity. By contrast, with the exception of a cowlick at the very top of my head, my own dark hair was flat, lifeless, no matter how often I combed it, every second day or so.

I tried to not meet her eyes but she kept at it and so I offered a half-smile, no teeth. It turned out that was impetus enough. She sauntered over to my table and stood above me. "Are you a writer?" she said chirpily.

"Yes."

"What do you write?"

"Fiction."

"You're very dedicated."

"Why do you say that?"

"Well, I see you are very absorbed in the story. You hardly look up from your work, from scribbling away."

Scribbling away? I had never in my entire life heard anyone use that phrase. What exactly did it mean? Scribbling entailed writing in a careless way, in a meaningless way. Was she trying to make fun of me?

"I'm actually writing," I said.

"Of course you are."

I would have preferred to be left alone at that point but the woman asked politely if she could join me. *Please* and *If it is no bother,* followed. I really had no choice.

"And what fiction is it you are working on?" she asked, bringing her coffee to my table.

There was something a bit off about the woman's language. She was French, no question.

"You have an accent," I said, pointing out the obvious. "From France?"

"Yes, very smart you are."

That was it, the extent of my social skills. I was in no mood for chit chat. "I have a deadline for this manuscript," I said, positioning my pen above the notepad I had been writing in.

"Yes, of course, you are a busy man. Please, I will sit here and drink my coffee and not bother you as you scribble."

"Not *scribbling*," I said. "Writing. Writing."

"Of course. Writing. Je m'excuse."

I returned to the project at hand but couldn't concentrate, feeling the woman's eyes burning holes through me. I put the pen down and crossed my arms. "Ok, so you want to talk. Why don't you tell me your name."

"Solange."

"I'm Karl. Anything else?"

Solange took a sip from her coffee. "You are . . . how you say it? Ah . . . intense . . . yes, very much."

I could tell there was no winning with this woman. So I gave up. "I'm finishing a story. But I can talk a bit."

"How come you are not using laptop? Everyone uses computer to write these days. Your pen and paper is very old-fashioned."

"I don't have a laptop," I said.

"And what is this story about, Karl?"

Ok, she asked for it. So I started to tell the woman about this paranormal story that I had only just started, the germination of the plot still very murky, but understandably got bogged down rather quickly. Solange's face gave it away, as if she had tasted a scoop of horseshit. It became all contorted upon hearing the word *golem*. Her forehead wrinkled, her mouth puckered, and her eyes opened wide with incredulity.

She had no idea what I was talking about. It was painfully obvious that in the telling of the story, I would first have to explain what a golem was. Fortunately, because I had read through *The Golems of Gotham* book and had become so enthralled, I had done my own research into what these creatures were all about. I felt confident enough to talk about them. "So to give you an idea, Adam, from Adam and Eve, was initially considered to be a formless creature, in effect, a golem. You understand? He was made from dust. Some arise from mud or clay but they're all conceived from the earth, that's a given. Actually, there are biblical references to golems but much of the literature regarding them seems to have come from the thirteenth century, mostly from Spain and Provence."

"Oh my, I didn't understand all the words you said, but enough, and this is so interesting."

"You think?"

I thought she was pulling my leg, that she would mockingly stick her finger down her throat. Instead, she seemed genuinely interested. "Yes, very unusual," she said. "And I also know this Provence very well. I have a friend who lives there."

"Do you want to hear more?"

"Pourquoi pas?"

I shrugged. "What did you say?"

"Ah, I mean, *why not?*"

"Very good. So it was in these regions of Provence and Spain that there arose something called the *Zohar*. It's also known as *The Book of Splendour*. It's not one book but a number of books and it is these books that are the foundational texts for the *Kabbalah*, which is the mystical aspect of Judaism."

"And this Kabbalah I know too. Movie stars wear such red strings around the wrist for protection against evil."

I had not heard of this and did not answer. But then, I couldn't care less about movie stars.

"Je m'excuse, not only movie stars," Solange said.

I took a hard bite from my bran muffin. "The Zohar speaks of very strange things. The relationship between ego and darkness, the nature of god and souls, cosmology.

So you can understand how something as bizarre as a golem might come from such writings."

"Again, very interesting, Karl. You speak of this strangeness very well."

"As I said, the Zohar was crystallized in the thirteenth century. But, it was written much earlier. According to legend, it was written in the second century by a rabbi. The Roman government was executing all Torah teachers and so this rabbi, along with his son, hid in a cave for thirteen years. It was there that he studied the Torah and, it is said, received divine inspiration from the prophet Elijah to write the Zohar."

"I think he would study so much because there is not so much else to do in a cave."

Solange's petty comment was irksome. Especially as she laughed when saying it. I had done so much research on golems that I felt my treatise deserved something better than an inane joke. Of course all this golem stuff was pure hokum, but as the words flowed from my mouth, it made me realize that if I told someone about the creatures, they could at least listen quietly and not spit out ridiculous comments. Here was an opportunity to reveal the full extent of my knowledge, and yet I was being constantly interrupted.

"Look, if you would like me ..."

Solange interjected. "Yes, please continue. Je m'excuse une autre fois."

I went to the counter for a refill on my coffee. When I returned, Solange was silent so I started again. "Anyway, between the second and thirteenth century, the Zohar seems to have gone missing. Nothing was heard of it. That's simply a mystery. I should say though that perhaps the most famous golem story occurred in the sixteenth century. It was called *The Golem of Prague.* The rabbi in Prague at the time—Rabbi Loew—constructed a golem from the mud of a river. There was a pogrom going on in the city then that was initiated by the Holy Roman Emperor Rudolf II, and the golem was brought forth to help vanquish the oppressors of the Jews."

Solange held up her right index finger.

"Yes?"

"Qu'est-ce-que c'est, 'vanquish'?"

Aside from the words "bonjour" and "allo," my French was almost non-existent. Given the context however, I surmised that Solange wanted to know the meaning of the word vanquish. I asked and was right.

"Vanquish means to beat down or conquer. I think that's the best definition. Usually we refer to this term when talking about war."

"I understand."

"Good. Now, the golem in Prague . . ."

"And what is 'pogrom,' please?" Solange asked. "I have not heard of such a word."

So I explained the meaning. How it referred to an ethnic cleansing of Jews. How they were being killed, their houses burned. Then I continued with the tale. "So in effect the golem was able to beat down the oppressors of the Jews. Rudolf II and his men. But, what happens with these creatures is that they become too powerful and are then difficult to control. So they have to be put down."

"You mean *killed*?"

"One might think so but remember that golems are constructed from the earth. Soil. So when they are put down, we refer to the fact that they are returned to the earth, to the ground from where they arose."

"Adam was made from this dust and soil, as you say. And we are from Adam. Eve too. So that means that people too are not killed, only put down."

Solange's running commentaries had reached their zenith and I closed my notepad and stood up. "I really must be going," I said.

"And why is there not some magic academy that can track these monsters to see where they are at all times? In *Harry Potter*, there are many wizards who can do this."

"Goodbye. It's been a slice."

"Will you come back for more scribbling, Karl? I am here very often at this time."

"We'll see. No promises."

"And just one more thing."

"Yes?"

"These golems, they are part of Jewish history, no?"

"Yes."

"Are you Jewish?"

"No."

"Then why are you writing about such a thing?"

I didn't bother answering. I just picked up my things and left.

***

It turned out that that was not the last I saw of Solange. I could have easily picked another coffee shop to write in but something brought me back to the one where I met her. That something, I knew, was that despite the fact that she had been able to push my buttons, I actually enjoyed being in her company. It had been a long time since any female showed any interested in what I had to say. It didn't hurt that she was slim and busty. And oh, that face. So we continued seeing each other every day during the week at exactly 12:30 p.m. and we started becoming friendly. Friendly, a concept I wasn't overly familiar with.

I learned that Solange was a kindergarten teacher in Paris. "Pour les petites," she said. I also found out that she was on a nine-month sabbatical here in Toronto, specifically to improve her English. She attended an ESL school near Yonge Street and Eglinton Avenue and lived with a family in the area.

To say that I actually did any work on the story during the visits was a stretch. I never picked up my pen. It was simply two people getting to know each other. Well, that was only partially true. I can't in all good conscience say that I revealed everything about myself. Some parts I made up. I told her I was a grad student working on my PhD in philosophy but that I was also a successful writer, having published roughly thirty stories in literary magazines. Furthermore, that the novella I was working on was a distraction from the rigours of my doctoral studies; because I was fairly well-established in literary circles, a publisher had requested that I pen a novella. The golem story. Why I felt inclined to lie was beyond me. Well, actually that's not quite true. I suppose it had to do with insecurity. A once-proud student enrolled in the university's PhD program, I was now a former student and also unemployed. So maybe not a good package to put forth.

I did realize that our friendship was running on borrowed time, to coin an idiom Solange was probably unaware of. She would be leaving Toronto sometime in the next few months. I wasn't exactly sure what I wanted from her but could say with certainty that I felt the pull of attraction. She was perhaps in her mid-thirties, and possessive of a nature one might certainly call "joie-de-vivre." I had almost felt that perhaps some of her joyfulness could rub off on me if I hung around long enough. The other thing is that it had been many years since I had slept with someone. I knew it was a long shot with her but at least there was that possibility. So one day, I invited Solange to my place for dinner and, much to my surprise, she accepted.

I borrowed two cookbooks from the library. I had no culinary skills, eating almost every meal out. Shawarmas, samosas, hot dogs, fries, burgers—those formed the bulk of my diet. There was a Vietnamese place on Spadina Avenue called Bun Saigon that I frequented quite often. The best bowls of pho. Good shrimp dishes also. Inexpensive. And a Hungarian restaurant on Bloor Street called Country Style Hungarian Restaurant was also on my radar. At home I *prepared* ... and I use that word loosely ... TV dinners, Kraft Dinner, sandwiches of sliced meats, peanut butter (often eating straight out of the jar), and cereal (especially Cap'n Crunch). Mostly, I munched on chips, chocolate bars, jellybeans, yogurt-covered raisins. I hardly knew what a vegetable was.

But, I was happy with my diet. Sure the food was bad for me, but it was quite delectable, and cheap. Even if something was a bit off, I could smother it with packets of ketchup. Yes, the liquid red nectar, sweet, savoury, good for what ails poor people.

On this occasion though, I tried to cook something up for Solange. And since I told her that I made a pretty mean lasagna, that was on the menu. Of course I had to explain to her, quite unsuccessfully mind you, how the word "mean" played into the business of cooking up beef lasagna. She understood the normal meaning of the word but was stupefied by the context in which I had used it. I explained it was an idiom, similar to the phrases break a leg, or, kicked the bucket. That only made things worse. Solange's English was quite good but she just didn't get English-language idioms yet. Still, it was all in good fun, I was simply thrilled to have the woman coming over.

Lasagna and salad. Wine. Dessert was asking too much from my limited culinary skills so I bought some Hungarian *Dobos Torte* from Country Style, a decadent cake filled with layers of chocolate buttercream and topped with a caramel glaze. A classic dessert.

On Sunday, two days before the dinner, I began preparing the lasagna. I didn't want to have any surprises with a botched meal hours before. That turned out to be a wise move. I had rarely used the inside of the stove, instead simply using the two burners on top. When I tried to turn the stove on, it wouldn't light. I would have called the landlord for help but didn't really know how to contact them; it was an obscure numbered company. Someone from the company always picked up my rent cheque the first of every month from my doorstep. That was the extent of our involvement. So I did the only thing I could think of: I scooted over to Goodwill and purchased a toaster oven. Fortunately, it was in working order and the rest of the food preparation proceeded without a hitch.

* * *

I boxed up all of the stuffed animals that littered the apartment. I had bought them at garage sales and they kept me company, bears and penguins, dolphins, rabbits, robins. So many. I had no idea what Solange would have thought about all the furry creatures littering the apartment but didn't want to take a chance that she might think I had reverted to a childhood state.

I'm also not sure what Solange was thinking when she showed up wearing a short black dress and a white silk blouse. I know what I was thinking about, however—I wanted to rip her clothes off the minute she walked through the door.

She kissed me on both cheeks and produced a bottle of French Shiraz. "Very beautiful wine for beef," she said. I showed her around the apartment, although in truth there wasn't much to show. I concentrated on the many books in my library and also a photograph tacked onto the fridge door. "This is me in front of my class, taken a few years ago," I said. "I was teaching a course on ancient philosophy. Plato and Aristotle. I was a TA Teacher's Assistant."

"The Greeks," she said. "I know them a little. Socrates spent much time in that market, the *agora*, lecturing to anyone who was willing to listen. And sometimes to people not so willing to listen." Solange let out a hearty laugh and I quickly joined her.

As the evening progressed, we talked about many things, my parents, her family, the school she was teaching at, the philosophy program I was supposedly now enrolled in, her hobbies, her interest in the English Romantic poets, how she's enjoying Toronto. I asked whether she was related to the famous French actor, Gerard Depardieu, and she replied that sadly, she was not. She was particularly curious about how my novella was to end.

"As I told you, Solange," I said in a clear voice, "these golems become too difficult to handle after a time. Then you must put them down. Back to the earth they go!" I pointed downward with my forefinger.

"They're like Frankenstein people. Frankenstein people made from earth and clay. Wow, Karl, you have an imagination. It's wonderful. I think you are very talented."

"I think everyone has some talent," I said modestly. "It's just that some people don't foster their talent."

"*Foster?*"

"Yes, it means to nourish the talent. You know, to work on it all the time so you become very good at it."

"Ah yes, now I understand. And now I have something to tell you. I don't tell many people."

"Ok."

"In France, we have a show on the radio—*Le Monde Étrange*—that always has very strange topics. Things like vampires and UFOs and maybe even golems, like you write about. I listen to it any time I can. It's so interesting. The world is very big and unusual. Many things we don't understand."

"*Le Monde Étrange?*"

"*The Strange World,* I think it is in English. Yes, I love that show. You know, if I could, Karl, I would like to go on an expedition one day into the jungle and find some strange creatures. Or maybe even create some creature … like some mad scientist."

"Wow, I never knew, Solange."

"Science is very interesting. But *mad science* is much better."

The lasagna was a big hit and we each had a second helping. I surprised myself, I could actually cook something. Solange was right about the Shiraz—it really was the perfect accompaniment to the beef lasagna. And the Dobos Torte was to die for, simply irresistible; after tasting it, Solange said I must absolutely take her to Country Style to try the rest of the food.

All of this, the food, the conversation, the wine, the friendliness I showed Solange, was leading to the moment when I leaned in close and kissed her. At first she seemed hesitant, almost unsure. I thought she might bolt from the apartment, she seemed that skittish. But after I withdrew following the initial kiss and told her some lame joke that we both laughed at, she relaxed and began to enjoy the affection. I twirled my tongue deep within her mouth but she gently pushed on my chest. "Not yet," she said, and I obliged.

***

That was the start of it. During the work week, Solange and I saw each other on Tuesdays and Fridays. Usually I would join her for lunch at a place called Hannah's Kitchen, close to the ESL school she was enrolled in.

I continued to cook for Solange, I didn't mind at all. Even enjoyed it. And much to my own amazement, I now became quite an adept cook. The toaster oven didn't hold much promise for cooking deep dish meals and so I asked the proprietor of the butcher shop downstairs for assistance with the apartment's oven. It turned out that all that was needed was someone to take a match to the pilot light. Go figure, I didn't even know there was a pilot light. So now that it was working, I began preparing roasted turkey and chicken with baked potatoes, stews. On the stovetop, I became somewhat skilled at soups—chicken, barley, mixed bean, and pea. Desserts were still in the exploratory stage and I messed up muffins, cakes and pies on a regular basis. Too much flour, too little sugar, not enough yeast, things didn't rise, the dough tasted bland, even raw, all that and more. Still, I did turn out an awesome apple crumble pie on one occasion and peanut butter chocolate chip and oatmeal raisin cookies on others. I used recipes, my blueprints for success, and chopped and diced, sautéed and braised. I wasn't afraid to try my hand at new foods and the idea that I might fail never entered my mind. I loved cooking for Solange and got enormous satisfaction knowing she was enjoying my creations. I'd look into her lovely brown eyes, staring at them as she ate. I'd see her smile. It was a happy dream.

I did have one habit related to food that she couldn't abide by though. I had had it all my life and just couldn't give it up. At the end of each meal, I liked something sweet. Usually cookies. I would take a cookie, usually an Oreo, and dunk it in a glass of milk. Oftentimes, I would hold it under a little too long, and drown it. The soggy cookie would sink to the bottom of the glass and I'd have to remove it with a spoon.

"Ecch," Solange would say, her face all scrunched up.

"You know that's what I like." I usually stood my ground while fishing for the remains of the Oreo with a spoon, like I was scavenging for sunken treasure.

"So North American. Nobody in France does such a thing."

"We're not in France." I smiled ironically.

"I will now close." And with that she'd place the palm of her hand across her eyes.

"You should see what happens to Cap'n Crunch cereal when it gets soggy. It's worse."

"Ecch."

***

Aside from my wretched diet, there was something else that I parted with—my slovenly appearance. There was no way to explain it other than to say that I now turned my interest toward my looks. Ah yes, my looks.

The truth was that I never took any real interest in my appearance. My wardrobe consisted of a rag-tag assortment of clothes picked up at Goodwill, Value Village, and the clothing donation box at the corner of my street that I found myself occasionally rummaging through. My socks never matched, my pants were far too short, sometimes too long, sweaters had holes. What did I care? I had always been a philosopher, a man of mind, so taking an interest in my looks didn't matter. Besides, I wasn't sure that fashionable clothes and a proper haircut (I cut my own) would change anything—

I was a tall, gangly sort, with a swarthy complexion, flattened hair and a cowlick at the very top that absolutely refused to be tamed ... it stood straight up like a mini, wind-swept twister. Being a philosopher, I sported a beard and moustache, a goatee of sorts ... the two seemed to go hand-in-hand. Well, I tried to, but my chin and upper lip sprouted only patchy stubble, which I kept anyway. I'd had the same pair of black glasses for so long, at least 20 years, that they had come back into fashion. I had to thank Harry Potter for that. But it was my look, the absent-minded academic, and I accepted it. I felt that appearances were deceiving anyway. Put me in nice clothes, and one person might suggest I was handsome. Yet a second would say that, while I was well turned-out in my fine duds, I was nevertheless ugly. Which to believe? Why would one perspective be any more real than the other? Put me under a giant microscope and the texture of my clothes, of my face, my hands, arms, and the like, would differ from what could be perceived by the ordinary eye. It was all very ambiguous.

But now, entirely owing to Solange, I tried to make myself look, well ... as presentable as I could. I went to a local barber for a $20 haircut; it was considerably better than cutting my own hair. I shaved and bathed regularly and even managed to tame the cowlick with lots of gel. As for clothes, I found that if I took my time to very carefully select them from thrift stores and the clothing donation box, I could look decent. And now I washed everything I bought; previously, that was not the case— I would simply put on the clothes, which led to a few nasty cases of flea bites. To complete the picture, I even bought an iron. And so in the selfies Solange was so fond of taking of the two of us, I scrutinized myself very carefully and was surprised ... I had to admit, I looked pretty good ... and it didn't take a microscope.

Of course, of paramount importance was that I now had a lover and my life became devoted to her. I thought about Solange constantly, the one firmament in my otherwise dismal existence. I even went so far as to ask her to move into my apartment. She declined though, saying that it was better for the moment to remain with her Canadian family. They had graciously allowed her to stay on and she was quite comfortable in their house.

If there was one regret I had regarding my relationship with Solange it was that my parents never got to meet her. They would have adored her, I have no doubt. *She's a lovely girl*, is what my mother would have said. *Marry her!* And while both my parents had been quite set in their ways, I believe Solange might have changed them, the same way she was changing me. She would have done so just through her indomitable spirit, where everything she imagined was possible, even without a lot of money.

***

On Saturdays and Sundays we found time to explore the city. The family she boarded with were particularly lenient, allowing her much time off. The weather had turned, warm gales from the south signalling the end of winter. It brought with it smells of animal droppings and damp pine needles. Here and there patches of green grass could be seen beneath the retreating snow.

We went hiking in the Rouge Park, where we saw a family of beavers frolicking. Seemingly at every step Solange would point out some earthworm or spider or field mouse and tell me that the park's floor was teeming with life. *Life upon life*, as she said. She lifted a rock and showed me the slugs and ants that resided underneath. At a pond, she revealed the water skidders that slid on the surface. Having grown up in the city, it was all rather new to me and had I been with anyone else, chances are that I would have been annoyed. I had never understood the attraction of nature and would rather have spent my days on a restaurant patio than interacting with the creepy-crawlies that inhabited the forest floor. To be certain, carrying a heavy backpack while trekking along trails held no interest for me and paled in comparison to having a cappuccino or espresso while reading a book in a café. There were secrets that nature held, ones I would never be privy to, and that was just fine with me. Besides, I had enough bugs in my own place. Once I had made a foray on my own into the countryside where I stayed in a cave for a while. And while that adventure was pleasant enough (although I was forced to kill frogs to eat, and steal chicken eggs from a farm just to survive), it was a one-off, never to be repeated. But now it was different. Walking with Solange made me want to understand the beauty and magic of things that were foreign, the hills and rivers, the insects, birds, and animals.

I brought Solange to the top of the CN Tower where she jumped on the glass floor, while I stood a good distance back. Looking down at the ground through a glass partition some eleven hundred feet high was not my idea of fun. But Solange revelled in it, making imaginary snow angels while on her back.

I rented a car for excursions out of the city. We drove to Niagara Falls, Stratford, and the quaint Amish village of St. Jacobs. There, we visited studios and galleries and famers' markets. We picked up jars of jam and jelly for her return to Paris. I noticed Solange carefully scrutinized each and every jar for ingredients. "My parents will love these," she said.

More than almost anything, Solange loved music and dancing. She could do it all—Jitterbug, Ballroom, Swing, Salsa, you name it. She had taken many dance lessons throughout her life and could move with the best. And that is precisely what she did—move. She told me that dance allowed her to let go, dispense with the mundane chores of the everyday. While I learned to accommodate her on her many interests, this one thing I couldn't. My body always felt firmly rooted to the ground, like I was wearing cement shoes. To appease Solange, I would accompany her to nightclubs. But when she pulled me on to the dance floor, I froze. She danced circles around my stationary body, vamping and mouthing the words to songs I didn't know. I tried waving my arms but became aware that I must look like a chicken flapping its wings, and so I stopped. But that didn't deter Solange. If I wouldn't, or rather, couldn't dance, she would bounce away from our table and find a group of similarly inclined women on the floor. Rhythm, sweat, the beat of the drums. They were in a zone and there was no entry for me, the man who had always been more attuned to the mind than the body. I didn't mind sitting it out, I loved watching Solange dance. But on one occasion, a man asked her to dance. She looked at me, I nodded, and away she went. They danced quite a long time. He was very adept, very slick, with all the right footwork. He dipped her, lifted her, and even flipped her in the air. I saw them laughing and my heart skipped a beat. I could barely breathe. My jealousy was almost unbearable but I just had to take it.

That one episode aside, I was having a blast. *A blast*: a word that had never appeared in my lexicon before. I did all these things for Solange but it was her enthusiasm for life that motivated me, that brought something out that I never knew existed—joy. Her motto, explained in a mix of English and French and hand signals, was that *you will never again be as young as you are today.*

We became lovers. I lusted for her daily and when not there, had to satisfy those urges myself.

If I had been a different sort of person, I might have never let her go. Maybe got on to my knees and proposed. But I wasn't. I was me, Karl Pringle, full of contradictions and insecurities, carrying around an entire Louis Vuitton set of heavy emotional baggage. I may have been an ok boyfriend but was definitely not marriage material.

And despite knowing that, I really didn't want to let Solange go. I understood, yes I knew, that I would never find anyone as good for me as her. She was so caring, so nonjudgmental, that it made me feel that I could do anything in her presence. Be more than what I was and let go of my checkered past. Every day I hesitated, unable to decide between who I was and who I aspired to be. During my worst moments, I wondered what Solange saw in me. Even when she told me that she thought I was handsome, very smart, highly creative, caring, I had a hard time believing her. I thought that if only I could embrace her vision of me, then maybe I could escape my fate. And all of this against the background of an hourglass that was running out. Only months remained before *ma petite amie* would be leaving for good.

As it turned out, a new complication was thrown into the mix, one I was hardly ready for. Solange came over one evening, a night she usually reserved for the family she was staying with. She appeared especially solemn and unsteady, like she would collapse from the weight of her burden. I offered her a drink of something warm, a tea or hot chocolate, but she asked for a glass of wine instead. She reached for my hands with both of hers and stared me straight in the eyes.

"I'm pregnant," she said.

***

It was my fault. I should have worn protection. It's just that I wanted to know her completely, warm flesh on warm flesh, deep within. Stupid, I realize. And yet, I felt I should be gentle with myself. Not overly critical. The woman had brought out feelings in me that I never would have imagined.

I bought a ring valued at $1,625. Diamond band with burnished brown 18k gold. I was never one for jewellery, thinking it to be adornment worn by the very vain, but had to admit this was a stunner. Elegant. I didn't have the money for it and put it on my credit card.

Now I did the unthinkable; one evening I got down onto one knee and offered Solange the ring. She gasped, and cupped her hands around my face.

"Karl, please get up."

"Solange, I'm serious."

"We need more time, Karl," she said. "We must talk."

"At least keep the ring." I put it on Solange's left ring finger.

"Oh Karl. Please hold it for now." She put the ring into my palms and closed my fingers around it. I could see that she was blinking back tears.

"Sit at the table," I said, holding out a chair for Solange. I made her tea, and toast with blueberry jam. I had been a wordsmith my entire life but now had none. I didn't know what to say, didn't know what to do. Now that I had a moment to collect myself, I realized I didn't really want to marry her and be a father. I had no instinct for those things, I just didn't want to lose her. But in the overall scheme of things, that meant nothing. Nothing. Solange was looking for love, and the only sort of love I had ever known my entire life resided in school, with philosophy, fiction books, and imaginary characters within those books. Even if my dearest told me otherwise, I knew I really had nothing to offer her.

"The baby, Karl. I'm going to have it. There is not so much time left for me."

I nodded. "Yes," I said, burbling.

"Soon I will be thirty-six. Not much time at all. My last chance."

We spent the rest of the evening just holding onto each other. She took the ring from my hands and put it onto her baby finger. Unlike when it fit snugly on the ring finger, now it moved around and around. "It's a better finger for now," she whispered. "And I can have the size changed."

A thunderstorm suddenly moved in, the air crackled with electricity, and the rain, whipped by heavy winds, pelted the windows. Solange and I sat on the sofa and looked out, safe within the confines of my tiny apartment but aware that Mother Nature had effectively trapped us inside. I didn't mind, I was with my lady. My pregnant lady who believed in the kooky things she heard on that French radio show *Le Monde Étrange,* including believing in me, maybe the kookiest of all things. Me, the failed philosophy guy, the failed writer, the failure at just about everything. As I reached for Solange's hand, it felt so strange that I had managed to pull the caper off. It came to me then, this song by the band Talking Heads—"Once in a Lifetime." Yes, about the man who has a beautiful wife and a beautiful house, and he wondered how he got them.

I looked over to the table. There was still some Oreo cookie at the bottom of my glass, sunken treasure. But I let it linger in its bliss, slowly disintegrating. I couldn't tempt fate, lest I wake up from the dream.

***

We met the next day and the day after that. Weeks passed. Although Solange realized it wasn't the right time to make any commitments to me, she also knew that she couldn't leave. Not yet. So she called her parents in France and told them the news. Then she called her school and asked for yet a further four months leave.

Circumstances had changed, she told them. Extraordinary circumstances, although she didn't elaborate further. Seeing as how she was a long-term employee, the leave was granted.

For my part, I made a concession as well. I gave up my writing persona. I told Solange that the book deal with the publisher had fallen through. *Artistic differences* was the way I put it. Money, the print run, editing, royalties, we just couldn't agree on terms. Her response was that it was a great shame, seeing as how talented I was. And that I shouldn't give it all up, there was a publisher out there who would love my work and with whom I would get along especially well.

***

All the things Solange and I had done over the past while cost me a small fortune. I was running out of money. My two credit cards were nearly maxed out. The only source of money coming in was the princely sum of $595 from Welfare. The one saving grace was a $6,750 bond that my parents, as poor as they were, managed to squirrel away for me. It was my only safety net and I was always reluctant to cash it. Now I had to. There was no way out though—I really needed to work. I just didn't want to be stuck in a dead-end situation. I wanted a job that was viable, where I could use my faculties, and one that would make Solange proud. That would make my child proud. But the odds were against me, I knew that. I was in my late thirties with only assorted jobs that never lasted very long, and underwhelming academic achievements on my resume.

My new work life began as a trainee in the claims department of an insurance company. The phone rang nearly every minute. Someone was unhappy about the repairs to their car, the settlement offered on their break-and-enter claim, the contractor who was late arriving to fix the water damage in their basement, even my tone of voice … this, that, and the other. The person who was in charge of my training seemed to abscond for large periods of time and so every day I tried to muddle through thirty to forty new pieces of mail. I lasted eight days.

My next job was as a taxi driver. The city roads were congested and I hated driving for long stretches with no passengers. I tried parking in front of a few hotels, hoping to get some decent fares to the airport but the doormen directed customers to airport limousines instead. On one occasion, an inebriated man threw up in the back seat; I had to clean it up. On another, two punks got into the cab, one in the front and one in the back. I took them seven blocks and they got out without paying. I wasn't about to chase them. I lasted five days.

I tried other things. Pest-control technician, for instance. But I quickly realized that sleuthing through houses looking for rodents was making me physically ill; I felt nauseous all the time. Three days. A better option was working in a hardware store. At least for four days. The problem was that I had no interest whatsoever in any of the products. I couldn't tell the difference between a ball-peen hammer and a tack hammer or understand why anyone would want either of those things.

When things looked especially bleak, my luck changed; it was the day I happened to be walking past High Park. The west end was another area of the city I rarely frequented. I was only in Bloor West Village visiting a French pastry shop Solange was so fond of. I bought a few baguettes and fine pastries and decided to walk back. Along the way, I noticed a sign tacked to a bulletin board at the entrance to the park. It said that *Parks & Recreation* was looking for part-time help. To apply within. So I did and much to my great amusement, I got the job on the spot. It so happened that the administrator who interviewed me—Istvan Bartus—had long ago been a friend of my father's back in Hungary.

It was laughable. I knew absolutely nothing about taking care of grounds. And yet, in some ways, the job suited me. Istvan allowed me to pick my own hours, and which three days of the week I wanted to work, so I chose the evening shift, starting at 6 p.m., and finishing close to midnight. I was to prune, weed, roll sod, trim the hedges, plant, empty trash cans, and pick up branches and garbage. If it rained, which it often did in the spring, I had to gather up all the worms I could find and deposit the whole squirming lot into a paint can on Istvan's desk. I never found out why he wanted them nor did I bother to ask. Maybe he sold them to fishermen, who knew? The public washrooms had to be cleaned and all graffiti scrubbed from the walls. There was a swimming pool that I was to keep an eye on, making sure kids didn't scale the fence for a quick dip. The training period consisted of two weeks, after which I was on my own.

One perk that came with the job had to do with the allotment gardens. For a flat fee of $30.00, the public could rent a plot of ground. They weren't terribly large, about twelve feet by seven feet, but for the avid gardener they did nicely. They were also much coveted, with long waiting lists. I was no gardener but Solange surely was. And because I was now an employee of Parks & Recreation, I was able to secure a spot of my own at no charge.

The arrangement worked out perfectly. I was to work three days. It allowed me to meet with Solange during her lunch hours at Hannah's Kitchen, and we also had the occasional weekend to ourselves. Some Saturday mornings we ventured to the allotment gardens.

"Plant low crops on the east, tall ones on the west," the old man who worked the plot next to ours said. "That way the morning sun will warm the soil." He certainly looked like the real deal—coveralls, straw hat, rake in one hand, trowel in the other. And according to Solange, who grew up on a farm, it was sound advice. She planted carrots and potatoes to the east and peas and tomatoes to the west. She also found space for zucchinis and kale.

*　*　*

Solange had insisted that I get a cell phone. She wanted us to be able to reach each other at a moment's notice. I hated the twits who walked around yapping loudly on their phones, subjecting me to their inane conversations about what they were going to have for dinner that night and other trivial details of their appalling lives. So I held my nose and bought one. The most basic phone imaginable—$29.95 for two hundred minutes a month. No texting, no picture-taking, no internet access. For Solange, I would do anything. It turned out to be prophetic. Because on an evening when I was working at the park, using a pressure washer to remove some graffiti from the outer brick of a washroom building, she called.

"Don't be upset, Karl," she said.

Starting a conversation that way was tantamount to giving me a good swift kick in the balls. It could only be bad. I immediately turned off the washer.

"I'm in the hospital," she said. I could hear her crying.

"Solange, what's wrong?"

The next voice that appeared on the line was that of Mrs. Sutherland, the woman whose house Solange was staying in. I had met her on a number of occasions and was someone I was quite fond of.

"Karl, it's Joan."

"What is it?"

"You should get here as fast as you can. Solange has lost the baby."

I left the pressure washer right there on the ground and sprinted to Bloor Street, where I hailed a cab. My stomach was in knots, my mind was racing, and each red light we stopped at seemed interminable. The driver started the usual small talk about the weather but I shut him down at once, telling him to just drive as fast as he could.

At the hospital, I took the stairs two at a time. In the room, Solange was surrounded by Joan and her husband and their two kids. June was holding Solange's hand when I walked in. There was nothing to say, nothing. I just embraced my girlfriend and held on, kissing her madly on both cheeks.

"I'm sorry," Solange said at last.

"No. no. There's nothing for you to be sorry about." I held her at arm's length and looked at *ma petite amie*. She was as beautiful as ever. Pale, clammy, but still beautiful.

A short time later, a nurse walked in and asked us all to leave; the doctor wanted to run some tests. In the hall-way, I corralled him, a black stethoscope hanging loosely around his neck.

"What happened?"

"Are you the husband?"

"Boyfriend."

"Most miscarriages occur during the first trimester," he said. "Women in Solange's age bracket have a one in four chance of miscarrying. But we don't always know why they occur. It's sometimes related to age but not always. Often there are chromosomal problems, a dam-aged egg or sperm."

"But there were no warning signs," I said.

Joan was standing nearby and interjected. "Actually, she was having some really bad back pains lately. She had also lost a few pounds. Maybe five or so."

"Those could have been signs," the doctor said. "Now if you'll excuse me."

"What are you going to do to her?" I asked.

"We had to do a procedure called a D & C to con-trol the bleeding and prevent any infection. It's fairly routine but we like to monitor her. You can come back tomorrow."

The doctor put his hand on my shoulder. "I'm sorry for your loss," he said.

Joan and her husband invited me to the cafeteria for some food, a tea or coffee, but I declined. I just wanted to be alone.

As I walked out of the hospital, I thought about the doctor's edict: *likely a damaged egg or sperm*. I concluded that it could only have come from my side. Solange was as healthy as a horse, from good stock. Whereas I had come from the underbelly of European civilization—Hungarian Roma. Silently I cursed my parents. Even from their graves they were tormenting me.

* * *

We held hands and went for walks. Solange's pain was palpable; I could sense it in every pore of her body. It wasn't anything she said; rather, it was what she didn't say. She didn't talk about the baby, not about her school friends, she didn't say much at all. On occasion, she would mention her kindergarten students and how much she missed them. And her horse Blondine. Also, the newspaper *Le Monde* and the magazine *Paris Match*. Most of all she missed her parents.

It shouldn't have come as any great surprise then, when she put both my hands in hers, held them to her cheek, and said that she was returning to France.

"You can't go," I said.

"Mon coeur est brisé," she whispered. "My heart is broken, there are no other words. So you must understand that I want to be close to my real life. I must go."

"I don't understand. Real life? Am I not real for you? And so, what about me? What about *us*?"

"I love you. But it's not enough."

"Of course it's enough," I said. "We can try again."

"No."

"Just that—*no*?"

"Yes, just that, Karl." Solange turned to look into my eyes. "You are such a good writer, you have forgotten. Maybe you should resume your work. Put your energy into that."

How could she say that? I let go of her hands. Let go of the woman I cared about, the only person I cared about.

"Here," she said, and handed me back the diamond ring I had bought her.

* * *

The days that followed her departure felt like the end of days. I was empty, emotionally crippled. My heart was heavy as a sack of bricks and I found myself just going through the motions. I would climb into bed and think of Solange. Only her.

I spent hours walking aimlessly through the streets, locked into myself. I met no one's eyes and no one met mine. I felt no connection to anyone, like I was an alien just landed. Life was just so unfair.

This went on for weeks, and with each one that passed, I felt more hopeless. I had stopped showing up for work but because of the circumstances, which I explained to Istvan, I expected that he would keep my job for me when I returned, But he hadn't, he had hired someone else. "I'll keep you in mind if something turns up but you have to understand that I didn't know when you were coming back," he said.

"That's the best I could hope for," I said. I laughed good-heartedly and shook his hand. I visited the allotment gardens and saw that all the vegetables Solange had planted had withered.

* * *

I tried to write. Finish the novella. For Solange's sake ... and mine. Maybe it would be my salvation. But when I sat down at the computer, I found I couldn't get past the first few paragraphs. I'd read what I had written and throw it out. I knew good writing from bad and this was definitely bad. I just couldn't write in an interesting way. Nothing flowed, I couldn't turn a sentence over. I tried mixing it up, using both the present and past tenses, first person and then third. Nothing. So with each failure, I felt myself sinking and would slump my head against the computer desk. It was sheer agony, nothing less, and old feelings of worthlessness began to creep in. I thought my brain would explode and I found I had to nap often during the day to keep myself sane.

The one thing that kept me going was a woman named Beverly. I had known her in grad school and I ran into her quite by chance at a café in Kensington Market, where I lived. We hadn't seen each other in years.

"I'm a writer," I told her. "I've had many stories published in magazines and now I'm working on a novella. A few publishers seem interested."

"What's the novella about?" she asked.

"Oh, it's about a mythological creature called a golem. Do you know what that is?"

So I told her. Told her about *The Golem of Prague*, Rudolf II, the pogrom, hiding out in a cave for thirteen years, the Zohar, Spain and Provence, and about golems having to be put down as they become too unruly. I told her everything I knew about golems. And not once did she interrupt me.

Beverly came over to my apartment and it was implicitly understood. Nothing needed to be said, it was just two animals in heat. Two animals in need. The sex was rough, the floor of the apartment littered in the morning with empty beer and wine bottles and condoms. After, she would ask me about writing—she wanted to try her hand at it. I told her the most important thing was re-writing. *Revise, revise, revise.* Polish the work until it shone like a cut diamond. I explained to her that she should write what she knew about, that all writing was, at least to some extent, autobiographical. I went on and on. "And don't aim for the stars," I said. "Start small, try to get your work into literary magazines. Not *The New Yorker*. My first story was with a very small magazine in northern Ontario, I don't even remember what it was called. It was a general interest magazine. Oh, one last thing: when you think the story is good, let it go. You have to know when something is finished." I told her the story of Joseph Grand, the character in Camus' *The Plague*, who has ambition about writing the perfect novel but can't get past the first sentence. He wants to shock the world with his writing but that first sentence is never quite good enough to shock. Standard stuff. I felt good about lying to Beverly regarding all that I knew about literature and writing, how I managed to climb to the top. Well, that I was on my way. And that was how it was, there was nothing left for me but to lie.

WHEN SHE LEFT

When my girlfriend Solange left me to return to France, without any forwarding address, I was beside myself. I missed her so much and didn't know how to accept the fact that I was alone, as I had been much of my life. I came to the conclusion that I should find her. Yes, find her and then ... Well, I hadn't got to that point yet. But something. Maybe beg her to marry me. Maybe stay in France and wait for her to come around. Woo her back. I didn't have it all figured out but needed to start somewhere. So I Googled *Private Investigators*. The whole cloak-and-dagger business was way out of my line of experience. All I knew about it was through the old *Barnaby Jones* TV series, in which a white-haired Buddy Ebsen played a P.I.

I was pleasantly surprised to find a private investigator named Sheila Greene who worked out of an austere office space on Dupont Street in the Annex, next to a dry cleaning shop. Right at street level, the place was inauspicious to say the least, there was no sign on the door and only two chairs and a black and white wall clock with overlarge numbers, the kind I distinctly remember from grade school. Tick tock, tick tock, went the second hand ... I had only just walked in and the sound was already driving me crazy, like it was ticking down the last seconds of my life. Behind a desk piled high with folders sat Sheila Greene, the simple black nameplate with white lettering giving her away.

"Come in Mr. Pringle," she said at once, extending a hand. "I've been expecting you." She was much more petite than I would have imagined. I suppose I had been expecting someone big and burly, someone with a holstered gun. As for me, I hadn't shaved in quite a few days, my clothes were rumpled, my black hair matted and unclean. I was a mess.

"I usually work on a contingency basis," she said straight off.

"What does that mean?"

"It means that you pay for certain expenses as I go along, like gas for my car, copies, phone expenses if long distance calls are required … things like that. But you don't actually have to pay for my services unless I find the person you're looking for. And get the information you need."

"And how much will this all cost me?"

"If I find the person, it'll be $1,000 in this case. You gave me some preliminary details over the phone, so I'm somewhat aware of how much work is required." Greene leaned far over the desk. "Can you afford that, Mr. Pringle?"

"I can afford that."

"Good."

"But what if you don't find her?"

Greene stared at me with steely-blue eyes. "I always find them," she said. "But, in the unlikely event that they elude me, you will only have to pay for my expenses."

"Ok, that sounds fair. Anything else?" The clock was driving me crazy and I had to get out of there.

"There's a $250 deposit."

I signed the prepared contract, wrote out a cheque that I wasn't sure would clear, and after Greene and I went over everything I knew about Solange, bolted out the door before another second could tick off.

***

Greene was as good as her word. Four and a half weeks later, she called to say that I owed her the remaining $750. Plus an additional $500 because she had spent more time researching the matter than originally thought. And that I wouldn't be disappointed. Like she told me previously, she always found them out.

I couldn't bear another moment in her office what with that dreadful clock, so I asked whether we could meet at a coffee shop. She agreed and came down to my neck of the woods, meeting at Wanda's Pie in the Sky on Augusta Street, simply Wanda's to everyone local.

"The best pies in town," I said. "I'll buy you one. What would you like?"

"Thank you, nice of you. Apple would be fine."

I came back with two pieces of apple pie and two coffees.

"Before we get started, Mr. Pringle, I should tell you that Solange says *bonjour*."

I blanched, I must have. I could feel the blood rush from my face.

"Relax, I'm only messing with you, Mr. Pringle. I never reveal my clients. I didn't talk to her."

The panic abated, I poured sugar into my coffee and pretended to be nonplussed about the ruse.

"But I will tell you one thing, Mr. Pringle. You're a total fuck-up, you really are. Now I don't know exactly why you asked me to track down Solange Depardieu but I will say this. If you are really interested in her, which I suspect you are, then you shouldn't let that girl out of your sight. Accept her love because she's a keeper and could be, if you let it, the best thing to ever happen to your miserable life."

I put down my cup. Why was this bitch giving me a lecture? She didn't know me, didn't know one godforsaken thing about me. She was just a stupid P.I. who probably didn't have the smarts to cut it in school. When all else fails, become a snoop.

"Excuse me ..." I said abruptly, trying to show her that I was in charge. "You know nothing about me. *Nothing.* So if you want to get paid, I would dispense with the derogatory comments and just tell me what you know about Solange."

Greene smiled knowingly.

"I always check out my clients. Rule No. 1 of the trade: Don't take any job for people you know nothing about. I don't work for shady people." She took a long sip of her coffee. "Now I wouldn't exactly call you *shady*. No, but what you are is a fuck-up, just like I said. You'd be surprised to know how much dirt I've found out about you, about your dismal academic background in philosophy, the many jobs you've been fired from or left, your continual collecting of benefits from Welfare. Other things too. Buying copious amounts of weed and sometimes other drugs from a dealer in the Market.

Buying stolen computer equipment. Oh, I know all about you, Mr. Pringle."

Greene was a first-class bitch. The fact that she had checked *me* out made me want to spit in her face. Grudgingly, I held my tongue. Now that the cat was out of the bag about my past, there was no going back. Her checking up on me was horrific, wretched, abysmal, spiteful ... any one of another half dozen adjectives. But I still needed to find out about Solange and in a steady voice that belied my hatred for Greene, I told her so.

The contemptuous woman sitting opposite took a slice of pie into her mouth, rolling it around on her tongue. "Mmm, excellent," she said.

"So what do you have? I'm paying you a lot of money."

"Mr. Pringle, there's a lot you should know."

"Then go ahead. God."

We were sitting at a table near a window and watched as a photographer took pictures of a bride and groom across the street. They were kissing, hugging, and mugging for the camera. On one occasion, the groom carried the bride in his arms across the street.

"Ever have those taken of you?" Greene said.

"What do you mean?"

"Wedding shots. Have you ever been married?"

I poured two creams into my coffee and stirred. "You know so much about me, why don't you answer that?"

"You've been missing out."

"How do you figure?"

"It's part of life. As you philosophers say, *an experiential part of living.*"

Great. Now I was being given a lecture from a P.I. about the best way to live, something I didn't need in the least.

"I'm not suited for that sort of thing," I said.

"You'd be surprised at what people are suited for."

"Look, I'm free and that's all I care about."

"So you're free?"

"As a bird."

"And what exactly are you free to do, Mr. Pringle? You have no job, no family, no responsibilities, nothing."

"If you want to know the truth, I have none of the sludge that bogs people like you down. If I want to say that the moon is made of green cheese, I can do that. Or if I profess that five plus seven equals one-hundred-and-five, I'm at complete liberty to do so. I'm a philosopher by trade and dabble in possibilities. "

The P.I. crossed her arms defiantly across her chest. "I suspect, Mr. Pringle, that you just spout out these handy little phrases from time to time but that inwardly, you don't believe a word of it. Of course, you would never admit to it but I have no doubt it's true. At some point, everyone is answerable to someone. And we're all answerable to ourselves."

Greene pushed her business card across the table at me.

Sheila Greene, MA Psych.
Private Investigator

That explained the attempt at playing Freud. But I wasn't impressed. If anything, my disdain for the woman grew. Psychology wasn't nearly as difficult a discipline as philosophy. And the universities were churning out putrid MAs in psychology all over the place. The fact that she had a job following people around was proof.

"My impression," Greene said, "is that your world is very small. That you exist within a three- or four-kilometre radius in the city and rarely venture beyond that. And the reason you wanted me to track down Solange is because underneath it all, you're desperately unhappy with how tiny that world is. You're a pseudo-philosopher and one without an audience. Finding her may open things up for you. At least that's your hope. Your salvation."

If I had had a gun, and knew how to operate it, I would have shot Greene in the space between her eyes, right then and there. It wouldn't have mattered that other patrons in the café witnessed the massacre. In fact, I would have gladly led the police to the body.

I didn't want to engage any further in this psychological profiling. I hadn't paid Greene a lot of money for that. So I simply said: "Enough. Just get on with it."

"Ok, it's all about Solange. I get it. That's what you really want to talk about." She took another sip of her coffee and said: "Fine. Here's what I can tell you." Then she began in one long monologue:

"Her mother died many, many years ago and her father absconded. Nowhere to be found. So Solange was put up for adoption. She lucked out, ending up with a fabulous family in Loir et Cher, about one-hundred- and-forty kilometres from Paris. Jean-Pierre and Geraldine Depardieu. They had inherited a farm in that region but that is another story, which I shall now get to.

"So before Solange's arrival, Jean-Pierre had been an account executive at *Publicis Groupe*, an advertising agency in Paris. The money was great but the hours long and the pressure high. On those occasions when he would visit his uncle's farm in the Loire Valley, his stays never failed to evoke in him pangs of discontent with his present life. He suspected that things could be so much different, if only he had the courage to make a change.

"Geraldine was no less busy in Paris. Blinded from an accident during her youth, she taught residents Braille at the Hôpital Quinze-Vingts during the day and pottery at night at a school for continuing education. An expert potter for many years, she had struggled against her innermost desire to give up her day job and become a full-time artist. The problem always came back to the same thing—money. Artists are the working poor, her family would always tell her. There was something else. She was fiercely independent, whether because of her handicap or not was difficult to say. But she railed against any notions that she was any less capable than others, any less able to be financially secure. That meant two jobs and long hours. Even when she married Jean-Pierre, she staunchly refused any suggestion that she should give up her day job and concentrate on her pottery. Her husband's salary would have easily allowed her to do so but she would absolutely have no part of it. So she toiled at the two jobs but inwardly wished she could concentrate all her efforts at the potter's wheel."

At this point, I interrupted Greene. "Is all this necessary? You're giving me tonnes of information that I probably don't need. And in fact, I've heard some of this from Solange herself. We're not exactly strangers, you know."

Greene looked at me as if I were the devil incarnate. "Don't you want to know what kind of woman Solange is? Where she's from? How she was raised?"

"I'm not sure."

"The other thing you should know, Mr. Pringle, is that women only reveal to men what they know they can handle. My suspicion is that the stuff Solange fed you was pabulum because that's what she thought you were capable of ingesting."

"Fuck." I banged my closed fist lightly on the table. But Greene seemed to be right—I didn't know all that much about Solange.

"Just let me finish, Mr. Pringle. Because I suspect that after what I'm about to tell you, you'll be running into that woman's arms. At least that's what you should do."

Greene was so daft that I couldn't bear arguing with her. I went to the counter for another coffee and sat back down with my brew, waving my hand for her to carry on.

"When the farm came their way after the sudden death of Jean-Pierre's uncle, Jean-Pierre and Geraldine couldn't believe their good fortune. Of course they were devastated by his premature demise but never had any inkling they were in his will. It was as if the man was looking down at them from heaven, lighting their path. They had always adored him and looked upon his joie-de- vivre and carefree lifestyle with envy, envy that was born of their own desires, their own unfulfilled long-ings. As I mentioned, they too had long wished they could summon up the courage to make the necessary changes to live in a more harmonious arrangement with their own souls."

I interrupted once more. This time because I was curious.

"So how did Geraldine end up blind?"

"Nice. Now you're interested, Pringle. I have your attention. Look, the story is that, when she was six years old, she had been standing at the bottom of a garbage chute in an apartment building when someone threw a bottle of acid down. Not only did the acid blind her but she suffered terrible scarring, mostly around her eyes and mouth. According to Solange, one doctor told her she should be thankful she was blind, the scarring was so bad. Imagine saying that to a little girl."

"I guess."

"Solange told me that over the years, Geraldine had a lot of corrective surgeries. Magic hands worked on her. A lot of good doctors. But the skin around her eyes was pulled tight, waxy, like it had melted. Nothing could change that. And interestingly, she had an eye made of glass. A blue one I'm told, to match her other, unseeing eye. Just for cosmetic reasons."

The thought of having a glass eye made me nauseous. *How would you put it in? Take it out? Clean it?* I didn't dare say as much. To filter the thought from my mind, I did ask what the couple looked like.

"Jean-Pierre about six feet in height, a few inches taller than Geraldine. Both have olive skin colour and full lips. And now that they're on the farm much of the time, their normal uniform is a pair of jeans, work boots that are scuffed, and plaid shirts that look like retreads from the Sally Ann. No pretentions in their little slice of land."

"And how old?" I surprised myself, I was becoming a regular Chatty Cathy.

"I guess they'd be in their mid-sixties now."

"And how old is Solange?"

"Thirty-six, if I'm not mistaken. It's a good age."

I wasn't sure what Greene meant by that last comment but let it slide.

"So back to the story. The farm that Jean-Pierre and Geraldine inherited is spread over twenty acres. They have a quaint sign attached to the front gate that says: *L'amour vainc tout.* Know what that means, Mr. Pringle?"

"I'm not up on my French," I said, eating the last of my pie.

"It means 'love conquers all'."

Sentimental crap. But as with the glass eye episode, I held my tongue.

"Anyway, so they run it pretty much the way it has always been run; that is to say, not in the manner of your typical farm. Jean-Pierre's uncle had been an artist and the farm was a place to paint and revel in solitude and nature, his Walden Pond. You do know Walden Pond?"

"P-l-e-a-s-e," I said. Greene was so annoying.

"The only real change to the place is that Jean-Pierre and Geraldine put in a rather extensive organic vegetable garden. That and the dozen chickens in the barn give the farm some semblance that it is being run by farmers. But nothing could be further from the truth. They're city people, Paris born and raised. I should also mention that Solange has a horse there. A three-year-old mare called Blondine. That's her baby. She loves riding her through the countryside and sometimes takes kids from the city to the farm to ride as well."

"What kids?"

"Well you know she teaches and sometimes some of the older kids from the school visit. But she also volunteers at a school for children with mental challenges. And it's those children who come. They ride the ponies —Blondine is too high for them."

I hadn't known Solange volunteered. I wondered why she never told me.

Greene nodded at me. "So inheriting the farm made it easier for Jean-Pierre and Geraldine to change. Both gave up their day jobs and started in new directions. Geraldine concentrated her efforts on setting herself up as a full-time artist, obtaining an agent, contacting galleries, doing exhibits, and generally getting her work out for public viewing. She had a kiln installed on the farm that allowed her to work out of the house. She still comes into the city one afternoon a week to teach pottery. And, as if all those changes weren't enough, she also began to supplement her artistic salary by starting her own line of jams and jellies."

"Jams, huh?"

"*Tante Mathilde: Confitures et Gelées*—that's the name. Pear-honey, fig, plum, of course strawberry. Oh, and uh, blueberry-lime, grape, and rhubarb. Seven in all."

"Nice, if you're into that sort of thing."

"Well, I hear the business is thriving."

"Still not impressed."

"Why am I not surprised? Anyway, as for Jean-Pierre, quitting his advertising job was, I guess you can say, a more traumatic move. It meant giving up a full-time salary in order to go back to school and work on a master's degree in art history, his first true love. But after some soul-searching, they both determined that they could live without Jean-Pierre's big salary, and still live well. In fact, they could live better, more peaceably. Through diligent investing they had managed to put away a tidy sum of money and since there was no mortgage on the farm, they knew they could make do. The final step was to well up the courage within to make the final break. Once they did however, they knew there was no turning back."

"Huh."

"I can tell you that it's an eight-room farmhouse. Five cats now share the place, mostly strays who wandered in and never left. Chickens roam freely in the barn next to two Shetland ponies named *Gloria* and *Mollie*. And then of course there's *Mitch*, Geraldine's seeing-eye dog. Golden retriever. And, oh yes, Blondine."

"A regular menagerie."

"I notice a little disdain in your voice, Mr. Pringle."

"I'm not really into animals. They need attention, and I have no such paternal instincts."

"*Paternal instincts?* Huh, that's a strange term to use. You mean, you have to take care of them, is that what you're saying?"

I wasn't about to answer Greene. She wanted to trip me up, it was obvious. So I just waited her out, my arms folded across my chest.

"Ok, look, I brought all this up because you should know that, after Jean-Pierre and Geraldine settled into the farm, they thought about adopting. I don't know the entire story about why they didn't have a child of their own, but it's not important. The point is that they were ready for an addition to their family and that's when they adopted Solange. It was serendipity, you might say. The timing was perfect at both ends."

Greene appeared pleased with herself. A slight smile curled her lips. She then excused herself and retreated to the washroom.

I looked absently out the window and contemplated the story to date. Suddenly I wasn't sure that I really wanted to meet up with Solange once again. For one, I had time against me. More to the point, I wasn't really sure I could offer her anything. She had had a rough go of it at first, just like me. But she had come out the other end a fine human being. Salt of the earth. Whereas I … well, who was I kidding? … I was a rogue.

Greene returned.

"Maybe that's enough," I said.

"Mr. Pringle, you haven't received your money's worth. There's not much more but you should really hear the rest."

My heart felt heavy, like it was weighted down with rocks. And Greene's insistence that I keep my ears open only served to make it worse. It was like she was my shadow, following me around and making me ingest the cold reality of my situation. And yet … and yet …the woman did not see it the same way. For as soon as I told her to begin, she said:

"I can sense you're despairing, but don't. Solange is a grand human being, but a human being all the same. Like many of us, she's looking for love … it's something that's eluded her."

"Don't despair? Is that what you said?"

Greene rested her elbows on the table and stared at me. "Yes, because people who go out of their way to contact others usually do so for reasons of the heart."

There was no arguing with this psychopath. She seemed to read my mind, the low-life.

"How would you know she's looking for love?" I said, trying to shift the conversation away from me.

"I just know. Call it female instinct."

"No boyfriend?"

"No. Ah, but she was married a few years back. Would you like to hear about that?"

"Why not?" I said quietly.

"Well, about twelve years ago, Solange found the true love of her life. He was a Lieutenant with the National Police, situated in Paris. Their daughter—Angeline—was born the following year. By all accounts, it was a wonderful marriage. Of course Solange always worried about her husband's job. She worried that, when she kissed him goodbye in the morning, that would be the last she would see of him. Now, as it turned out, her fears were misplaced. But only slightly. For you see, Mr. Pringle, he did die. Not on duty as had been her concern, but rather in a car crash. The driver who caused the accident was going the wrong way. He was drunk. It happened along the *Autoroute du Soleil*, a rather ironic name for a highway."

"Like I told you, my French is bad."

"It translates to *Highway of the Sun*."

"So Solange must have been inconsolable."

"You don't know the half of it, Mr. Pringle. Because her husband was on his way to see his in-laws in the Loire Valley, Jean-Pierre and Geraldine. Solange was busy and stayed behind. But he had a passenger with him. Two dead in the car."

"You mean ..."

"It's true. Their daughter died in that accident."

I had nothing to say. The story exhausted me. I couldn't bear to hear another word.

"Nobody ever gets over those sort of things, Mr. Pringle," Greene said. "You just somehow manage."

I shrugged. There wasn't much else to say. I wondered how this low-life of a P.I. had obtained so much information, and so I asked her. Her answer was somewhat murky, mumbling something about having her own way of doing things. Undoubtedly she had managed to contact Solange and garnered her trust. That seemed to be a given although I had no way of confirming it.

"Do you have her address?"

"I wouldn't be a very good P.I. if I didn't at least have that, now would I, Mr. Pringle?"

I began writing out a cheque for the remaining $1250 when Greene reached across the table and touched my hand.

"It's only $750," she said.

I looked at her.

"I never meant to actually charge you more than the original contract price. I just wanted to know that you were serious about locating Solange. That your intentions were good. Like I mentioned to you earlier—*I was only messing with you.*"

I didn't understand any of it. Especially when Greene once again pushed her business card in my direction. "If you ever want to talk . . ." I turned the card over and there was written Solange's address.

***

I wanted Solange back in my life and I figured there was only one way to do that—go to France and talk to her. Beg her to come back to me. Explain why I was a perfect match for her. The only match for her.

I packed three shirts, three pairs of underwear, three pairs of mismatched socks. I took one pair of jeans, which I would wear constantly. I stuffed everything into a backpack. Just carry-on luggage. I had no idea where I would stay but thought I would figure it out when I got to Paris. Same with travel from Paris to Loir et Cher, where Solange lived ... I'd just figure it out later.

On the plane, I kept replaying in my mind what exactly I would say to Solange, how I would win her over. But I came up with a blank ... I didn't have much to offer, no matter how I spun it. So I settled down in my seat and watched a movie—*Back to the Future*. And as the movie neared its ending and we drew closer and closer to Paris, I became more nervous, thinking I had made a terrible mistake. If I could have, I would have gone to the pilot in the cockpit, put that gun that I used to obliterate Greene to his head, and told him to turn the plane right around.

I was bone-tired when the plane touched down and the first thing I did was take a taxi from the airport to Les Deux Magot, the very famous café in the Saint-Germain-des-Pres district. I had read all about it, how it has played an important part in Paris cultural life since the late 19th century, frequented by many important painters and writers and yes, philosophers too ... André Gide, Rimbaud, Hemingway, Sartre, Simone de Beauvoir, Picasso ... so many. I sat on the patio, watched people go by, and had a strong coffee that was sprinkled with a dusting of cinnamon. I was famished and ordered an open-face goat's cheese sandwich and a green salad. 16.50 the menu said but I couldn't tell if that was in Euros or USD. Whatever, it wasn't cheap. Visa was really good for something.

The sun was setting and I took a taxi to Shakespeare and Company, the legendary bookstore located on Paris' Left Bank overlooking Notre Dame Cathedral. From my reading on the 'net, I knew the bookstore was opened by

Sylvia Beach in 1919. Closed in the 1940s under threats of Nazism, it was reopened by George Whitman, who moved it down the road. It was a gathering place for many famous writers—Hemingway, James Joyce, Scott Fitzgerald, Djuna Barnes, Gertrude Stein ... like Les Deux Magots, the list of the very famous who frequented it was endless. It was home to the Lost Generation in the 1920s and the Beatnik generation in the 1950s.

As I entered the bookstore, I saw a sign on the wall:

**BE NOT INHOSPITABLE TO STRANGERS,
LEST THEY BE ANGELS IN DISGUISE.**

Ok, that was a good start.

Nobody had ever accused me of being an angel, but I was a stranger. They had to be nice to me.

I walked up to the front desk where a pretty blonde woman with a pixie cut was sitting and sorting through what looked like a stack of invoices.

"Hi, I'm Karl," I said, a bit breathless. "Just arrived from Canada. First time in Paris. I need a place to stay and read online that you have some bunks here."

'That's true. We allow people to stay over. Usually writers. Are you a writer?"

"Actually I am."

"What have you written?"

"I'm working on a novel about the relationship between a Canadian man and a French woman and how the long distance creates problems for them."

"Ok, you can have a bunk upstairs. You're officially one of our Tumbleweeds."

Tumbleweeds? I would later find out that that was the name given to those who stayed overnight at the bookstore.

I trudged upstairs and immediately bedded down, I was so exhausted. A black cat jumped on my chest and began purring. I didn't mind at all. At least something was happy to see me. I spent the next few nights at the bookstore and during the days, made excursions to The Louvre, Notre Dame Cathedral, the Eiffel Tower, Pere Lachaise Cemetery, and the Musée d'Orsay. I saw a cabaret show in the Moulin Rouge and a fabulous exhibit featuring art forgeries, artists who duped the world. Fake Picassos, Vermeers, Chagalls, Degas, Giacomettis, Breughels. A number of others as well. I didn't know much about art, but these fakes sure looked genuine to me. Fascinating.

In no time at all, I had spent three whole days sightseeing and only had a day and a half left until my plane was to go back to Toronto. It was a three hour train ride from Paris to Loir et Cher and I decided I would take it first thing the following morning. It was all going to work out just fine, I was now in great spirits. In the late evening I settled down on my cot and, surrounded by a large library of books, looked out at Notre Dame Cathedral. It was breathtaking. So beautiful.

The next morning, after a breakfast of a cappuccino along with two croissants stuffed with apples, walnuts, cheese and ham, all drizzled with honey, I took a taxi to the train station, bought a return ticket to Loir et Cher, and took my seat on the train. I pulled out a book I bought from Shakespeare and Company—*Perfume* by Patrick Suskind. A strange and disturbing tale about a depraved young perfumer who attempts to create the quintessential perfume by murdering women and lifting their scent. I had read the book previously, many years ago, and found it to have a strange, captivating hold on me. The main character *Grenouille*, has no personal odour but his sense of smell rivals that of a bloodhound. I recall that he was born in a cesspool of a food market to a mother who abandoned him; it appeared then that he had no chance. And so contemptuous was he of his fellow man that he retreated to a cave for seven years, far removed from the smell of humans. Set in eighteenth-century Paris, I thought that, if nothing else, it was timely to read a book set in Paris, the City of Lights, even if it was a very bizarre book.

It started raining heavily, streaking the window. I leaned my forehead against it and watched as the countryside rolled by. I felt sick, my stomach a bit achy. Whether from the ham and cheese sandwiches or just from nervousness, I didn't know. I closed my eyes.

When we arrived at the station at Loir et Cher, I sat in a chair for a long time, trying to collect myself, breathing heavily. I had come a long way, a very long way to a mythic world. A world of farms and horses and jams and blindness and art history and vegetable gardens and, of course, an ex-girlfriend.

It ended right there, in that plastic green chair in the train station. And who could blame me? Sitting in that chair, breathing heavily, I realized that Solange had become a rumour, a fleeting memory from my past. Yes, now she was just that, nothing more. I twisted the *Perfume* book in my hands, wringing it until all the pages were bent and distorted. Then I threw it in the trash bin and waited for the next train back to Paris.

BROKEN DREAMS

I had it all figured out, and it was going to be like this: I was going to meet with all my philosopher friends a couple of times each week at a café. We would talk philosophy. Debate philosophy. "It's not that way at all," I'd say. "Shape up." We all had thick skins and were fast friends so telling someone to shape up didn't matter. And we all admired each other anyway. So we'd drink strong coffee, smoke Gauloises, nibble at apple strudels, and laugh all day long. At the table next to us were the painters, all of whom wore black berets. And further along the way was a table full of writers. Serious students of literature. That was how it was going to be. But it never turned out that way. For one thing, I mucked about in grad school for many years until I was summarily kicked out and never realized my dream of getting a PhD in philosophy. And the other was that I was a loner by nature, so that café, full of interesting talents, special and charming associates, geniuses in fact, dissipated in a puff of Gauloises smoke. Maybe all for the best anyway. The poverty that pervaded the lives of all these *artistes* would probably have been too much anyway.

***

Plato once said that that in every one of us, even in the most moderate, there was a type of desire that was terrible, wild, and lawless. Something like that anyway. He was right. I only needed a little push for that desire to come out. That push was the magic mushrooms that I scored in the streets of Kensington Market where I lived. Powerful stuff, those shrooms gave me lucid dreams and made my head spin. Taking them, I found myself wanting to get out of my tiny apartment more and more. Go outside and simply stroll. Yes, jaunty strolls, with no destination in mind. There was a Latin phrase that I liked—*Solvitur ambulando*—which translated to "solved by walking." I felt that everything could ultimately be solved if one walked long enough. Even my wretched life of poverty and loneliness. One without goals and direction.

One night, after my indulgence into shrooms and while walking along grungy Parliament Street, a woman asked me for a smoke. I handed her a cigarette and as she stood smoking, told me that I looked lonely. That I could use some company. I looked around, to my left, to my right, and when I saw that no one was there, I walked with her into an alleyway.

"How much?" I said, squinting my eyes as I surveyed the woman. Her head seemed to morph as I was standing there and very soon, I was convinced she resembled a gargoyle.

"Depends what your pleasure is."

Her blouse was sheer and her nipples showing. My eyes narrowed and my anger suddenly bubbled to the surface. For an instant, I tried to repress it by turning away, but it was too strong, I felt overwhelmed. Before I knew it, I was hitting the woman with my balled-up fist, drawing blood. She let out a scream of shock and fought back but I hit her harder still, until she lay unmoving on the pavement. Her eyes were shut, her face bloody and swollen, but she was still breathing. I bent down low to smell her perfume. My head swirled. So exquisite. I inhaled and was suffused with lingering gossamers.

"Serves you right," I whispered. "Maybe next time you won't wear such a provocative blouse. And look like such a freak. A monster face, my God." Then I stood up and rushed off to a corner of the alley to heave.

***

I should have gone to the hospital but didn't. The woman had somehow bitten my hand and broken the skin during the assault. I figured a doctor in the emergency room would call the police. But I was in so much pain, my head reeling, I simply had to get treatment somewhere. So I went into a nearby walk-in clinic.

"It was a bar fight," I told the doctor. "I'm not a violent person but the guy was all over my girlfriend. I was worried about her safety. Anyway, I didn't think the injuries were too, too bad. The pain though, it really hurts."

"You're lucky you came when you did," the doctor said. "You were starting to lose circulation."

I was given a tetanus shot and stitches closed the wound. Gauze was wrapped around and around my hand and I was handed a couple of Tylenol 3s for the pain and a prescription for antibiotics.

Back home, I made bowls of instant oatmeal and sliced banana, eating absently with my mouth half-open. I had no strength to chew and only ate a wee bit, throwing the rest into a garbage bin. Then I drank from a quart of milk; it had been in my fridge a very long time and had soured but I didn't care, I needed the liquid nourishment. If nothing more than to rid myself of the drugs. I wasn't in my right mind when I hit that woman, I knew that. Like I told the doctor, I really wasn't a violent person.

* * *

The lure of drugs was powerful, especially when I was bored or suffering from an anxiety borne of the knowledge that I was a total failure. Weed was my normal drug of choice but having tried the shrooms, I realized I sometimes needed them. Needed the euphoria. The mind-blowing change of reality.

Fuelled by drugs, I walked alone along the streets in one of the most wretched areas of the city, St. James Town. There was a lot of public housing, many men's shelters, and hordes of miscreants working the streets. Wherever one looked, chaos appeared ready to take hold. A fight. A bum pleading for money. A mother screaming at a belligerent child. Someone being thrown out of a bar. I got swept up in the maelstrom, my brain whirring from all the commotion and from the drugs I had just taken.

I approached a woman. She was only a teenager, belying the gobs of black eyeliner and blood-red lipstick. Still, a true seductress. We spoke, briefly. "$20 up front, the rest when we finish," she said. "I'm no charity worker."

"Fine with me. I don't expect anything for free."

She led me through a dismal tavern that reeked of beer and smoke, and up winding stairs to a small room. She unzipped her skirt, then removed her blouse. Suddenly I felt terrified and had no idea what to do. I swallowed hard and remained standing, fully dressed. The woman looked at me with disbelieving eyes. "One of those, huh," she said, shaking her head. "I should have known. A mama's boy." She pointed a crooked finger. "Look, I ain't no social worker."

Mama's boy? That's what you're saying? So I hit her. My fist against her jaw. She fell backward against the bed and screamed bloodcurdlingly, her eyes now wide with fear. I set upon her at once, biting at her stomach and breasts, drawing blood. The blows rained down, one after another, I couldn't stop.

She kicked at my groin, which caused me to double over. Then she reached for a buzzer on top of a night table. That was it. Very quickly, I was jumped by two burly men who burst through the door, pummelling me with fierce punches of their own. My mouth spurted blood, my eyes ballooned and started closing, the world receding into a tiny speck. Somehow, I managed to squirm free and made a mad dash down the stairs. They followed, I could hear the clatter of their footsteps, but I was running for my life. It was no contest.

In my apartment, I collapsed onto the sofa. *Mama's boy, huh? Mama's boy.* The words assaulted my ears. I squeezed my eyes shut and my whole body began to shake violently.

After lying there for what seemed like hours, there was a loud knock on the door. At first I imagined it was the brothers. Them again. But then I heard the shouting.

"Toronto Police! Let us in!"

I stumbled to the front door and threw it wide open, gesturing with a magnificent sweep of my arm.

"What took you so long?" I said.

* * *

My cellmate was named Loco. He was too. He told me he was a full-patch member of the Rock Machine motorcycle gang, but I doubted it. To me, he looked like a biker wannabe, maybe a small-time hood. Big paunch. Thick arms and legs. Tattoos. But you could never tell; maybe he was a true biker. He would often give me the once-over without blinking, like he was sizing me up as to whether he could take me. I couldn't risk it, he might have been truly crazy. So I told him I shared his aversion to people, they were almost all moronic. "Women are the worst," I said. "They make you crazy with lust and then leave you." Loco liked that and nodded his big head, the same one that he would occasionally bang against the wall. Back and forth … back and forth … knock knock, like a woodpecker … day in and day out. Sometimes he drew blood. Then tasted it using his meaty fingers. I told him that if I had the chance I would live on an island in the South Pacific … alone. Just me and some palm trees. Or coconut trees, whatever grew there.

However clever I tried to be, it wasn't enough. I couldn't play the game long enough. For one thing, I had to share a toilet with Loco. No privacy. He would intertwine his huge fingers and stare at my genitals. And when *he* went, it was all gas and mind-numbing groans.

Hands to the head like he was contemplating the state of the world, eyes closed. Shits that were seemingly orchestrated, drawn out like one-act plays. Standing to pee, he would sometimes miss the bowl. There were puddles all over the floor and the guards gave me a mop and pail to clean up. Me!

When Loco wasn't banging his head or relieving himself, he would sometimes walk up to me and say: "You like to beat up little girls, huh? That's what I heard. Word spreads fast in this joint. Well, I can beat the shit out of you. When the time's right, just you wait and see." Very methodically, he'd pump his fist into his open palm. Sometimes he'd spit at my feet. "You think you're a bad guy, you ain't seen nuthin'."

One day he would be my best friend, the next he would threaten my life. No matter what I said, no matter how much I placated him, he would forget and change stripes. He was a certified nutjob, I was sure of it. I wanted to talk to the guards but worried that might set off my cellmate. Besides, I had no bruises. I also knew they didn't care what happened to me.

This all went on for two weeks, at the end of which I was thoroughly psychologically beaten down. I could no longer speak, I could no longer eat, I could no longer sleep. I was in a dank, stifling cellar, a wasted rat trapped underground. I just lay curled on my bunk and rocked, locked within myself.

* * *

I was moved to the prison's hospital ward. I was grimy from going in my clothes, shit and urine all over my legs and bum, so two male attendants carried me to a shower stall and propped my body against the wall. The water rained down, thousands of tiny body blows. I couldn't wash; my body had turned to stone. I just stood ramrod stiff and accepted the assault. The attendants yelled at me to clean myself but I couldn't; my arms wouldn't work. Only when one smacked my face with an open hand did I comply. Very slowly.

Everything felt like an abstraction, nothing was real. A psychiatrist was brought in to do an assessment. *Severe clinical depression* was the diagnosis, I heard him tell a nurse, most probably brought about by drugs. "He won't eat. He spits out every pill. He may be suicidal. Start him on IV. Lorazepam."

I was "formed," which meant they gave me a hospital gown and plastic slippers. I suppose they didn't want me running away. *Running, hah!* I could barely lift my legs.

They put me in a stark cell, this time by myself. It was barren and had no windows and, even when I was wearing my slippers, the floor felt ice-cold. I asked one of the attendants about moving to a better place, something not so cold, maybe a bit more homey. I actually used that word, homey. He laughed. "You'd better get used to it," he said. "This ain't the Ritz."

Shortly after I arrived, the same attendants escorted me down the hall to a large room, as sterile as an operating room. The light was blinding and I had to shield my eyes with the back of my hand. As I gradually grew accustomed to the brightness, I could make out many bodies lying inert on crisp white-sheeted beds. They were unmoving, occasionally moaning. They seemed drugged, long drools of spittle emanating from open mouths.

The sonorous hum of machines permeated the room. That sound infiltrated me, to my very core. It reminded me of a verse I had once read, a verse from George Eliot, the writer. *Middlemarch*, yes that's it. It was a small miracle that I could still recall. But I had often carried the book around with me, in case I ever needed something to read. *"If we had keen vision and feeling of all ordinary human life, it would be like hearing the grass grow and the squirrel's heart beat and we should die of that roar which lies on the other side of silence."*

My hearing was so acute, it was like listening to the grass grow. To die then of the hum! I managed to prop myself on my elbows to have a better look. Situated on the white-enamelled night tables next to many of the patients, the rectangular black machines showed a tangled web of white and red and black lines, little cobbled hills and valleys that paraded across the screen. But what was even more disturbing was the honeycomb-like cream-coloured wires that sprouted from the heads of the ghouls, the wires in turn connected to the odd-looking machines. It gave them the appearance of space beings. I wanted to ask the nurses what it was all about but my ability to control my own body had vanished. It had turned to rubber. Almost as quickly as I sat up I was back down, flat on my back.

Masked doctors in pristine white lab coats marched in. They moved me from my bed onto a metallic gurney and I was then wheeled into an operating room. The room was unnaturally cold. They slipped my body off the gurney onto a table.

"What are you looking for?" I heard one of the doctors say. I didn't understand what he was asking of me.

All I could think of saying in response was; *Please don't hurt me.* But I couldn't speak.

"What we look for," another doctor said, "is excitation of large numbers of neurons. The excitation builds and quickly overwhelms any inhibitory mechanisms that hold the neurons in check. And when that happens the brain gets swamped. Cerebral blood flow increases dramatically. We monitor the electrical signals using EEG."

Please don't hurt me.

An IV was put into my arm, just like when I was first brought into the hospital ward. I was told to bite down onto a rubber block; it tasted like chalk and I wanted to gag. A plastic mask was placed over my mouth and jelly was rubbed onto my temples. I could feel something being connected there. Then I was asked to count backward from one hundred ...

I woke up back in my cell, strapped to the bed. A nurse wiped the drool from my mouth and adjusted my helmet. I tried to tell her that my jaw was incredibly painful but no words emerged from my throat; it was like I was sinking in a mud puddle. A short time later, my nose began to bleed.

Two days later, I was jolted once more. For the rest of the day, I was utterly confused and could not remember my name. My limbs ached and again my nose bled.

The following day, as I was being taken from the room, aware of where I was going, I began to cry.

"Life is tough," one of the attendants said. "You made some bad choices in your life that landed you here. That's your fault; you can't blame no one else. And like I told you before—you just have to get used to it. This ain't no hotel."

In all, I was given six unilateral electroconvulsive treatments over a period of a week and a half. Interestingly and unlikely as it seemed, I responded fully. My depression went into remission and I began to eat voraciously. Surprisingly, the food was rather good. I half-expected watery fish soup, a piece of stale bread, but no, there were fried potatoes and an omelette. Potatoes ... and an omelette filled with green peppers, onions, I think some cheese ... and other stuff. Who would have thought! There was a plastic fork and knife but I shovelled everything into my cavernous mouth with oily fingers, and asked for seconds. And I slept, sometimes for ten or twelve hours at a stretch. I felt happy, even gregarious. I greeted the nurses with great big smiles.

Weeks went by, and then months. I did jumping jacks, push-ups, ate everything they offered, took my meds, slept or relaxed on my bunk much of the time, and tried to engage the guards in idle chitchat about the weather or their families. Generally, I was quite happy with the arrangement ... it was all silky smooth. And then there was an early discharge for good behaviour. Why not? I was the ideal prisoner.

***

Like I said, I had it all figured out. But it didn't turn out the way I wanted. It was my only chance, the friends, the café, and I still longed for them. The dream. It's just that being a philosopher wasn't panning out. For a time, I even thought that maybe I could give up philosophy and go to Paris and become a painter. Go to museums. Wear a black beret. Then I realized that, no matter where

I went, I wouldn't be able to get away from myself. I would probably be saddled with depression and anxiety and loneliness my entire life, even if I lived in Paris. I had read many an article over the years about the propensity for creative people to suffer from mental disorders. I was a philosopher, but maybe had some hidden creative talent. I had always hoped so anyway.

But of the creatives who suffered miserably, the list was quite long. Edgar Allen Poe, for instance, was beset with depression, grief, and delirium at various times in his life and his writings are replete with themes of madness, disease, death, necrophilia and entombment. And although I was no big fan of poetry (it was a discipline I didn't read, considering it to be a waste of time), I knew that many of the same afflictions possessed the poet Sylvia Plath. I had read her book *The Bell Jar* as a freshman in university and vividly recall she suffered a mental breakdown that led to a suicide attempt. During that time, she wrote that she hadn't washed her hair for three weeks, hadn't slept for seven nights. Her rationale for keeping her hair in a state of decrepitude was that it seemed silly to wash it one day, only to have to wash it again the next. Although her initial suicide attempts failed, she finally succeeded by gassing herself to death in her own kitchen. And the prose writer Virginia Woolf had mood swings throughout her life, eventually filling her coat with heavy stones and walking into a river, never to be heard from again.

Of course, the list of philosophers who were similarly afflicted was equally long. I knew them all from my studies. My hero, Friedrich Nietzsche, for one. In the late 19th century, he collapsed on a street in Turin and, it is said, never returned to full sanity. It may be solely anecdotal, it may not, but the collapse that precipitated his downfall was caused when he witnessed a coachman whipping a horse and threw his arms around the animal's neck. Syphilis and a hereditary stroke disorder, even a suspected tumour, may all have complicated the picture, but there is no denying that he was unbalanced.

Another philosopher that exhibited mental health issues was the father of existentialism, Søren Kierkegaard. He could never overcome his tendency toward depression, although indications are that he wanted to. He considered his black moods as a failing, saying that individuals in that state had the possibility of something greater if only they could get rid of the black albatross, the very one that followed Kierkegaard everywhere. He was quoted as saying: *"My depression is the most faithful mistress I have known ..."*

Michel Foucault was tormented with acute depression, Martin Heidegger had a nervous breakdown. John Stuart Mill suffered from melancholic depression. And so it goes.

* * *

Dreams, huh. They never seemed to work out. At least mine didn't. And I wondered if it was because, while it was fine to dream about things, you also needed to be grounded to realize them. I had to dutifully admit that I never was, my feet never securely touching the earth. It was like Marc Chagall. I loved his work. In many of his paintings there was no gravity to weigh people and animals down—they floated on rooftops or moved about freely through the air. In one in particular entitled *The Green Violinist*, the violinist seems to be floating just above the small rooftops of the misty grey village below. That was me, a lover of Chagall, and a floater, ready to be painted onto a canvass.

ACKNOWLEDGEMENTS

I'm grateful to Michael Mirolla and the rest of the Guernica Editions team for believing in this book's possibilities and helping to shape it. Also to David Moratto for the exquisite cover, showing a snapshot of bohemian Kensington Market. And to Julie Roorda, who was as fine an editor a writer could hope for.

There have been a number of people whose encouragement has been essential to the creation of this book but I'm especially thankful for my dear friends Richard Davis and Ann Fetherston for their unwavering guidance and support, without which this collection might never have seen the light of day. Similar kudos go out to friends Dawn Michael and Ken Martin.

I'd like to thank authors Lori Hahnel, Sharon Hart-Green, and Guglielmo D'Izzia, for taking the time to read these stories and compose wonderful blurbs.

I would be remiss if I didn't acknowledge the late George Whitman of fabled Shakespeare and Company, who long ago, when I was in Paris and one of his renown "tumbleweeds," greatly encouraged me to give fiction writing an earnest try.

Finally, I'd like to acknowledge all the wondrous readers of the world, who, with their deep love of the written word, keep the magic and sparkle of a writer's imagination alive.

ABOUT THE AUTHOR

Originally from Montreal, **Jerry Levy** currently resides in Toronto where he is happily retired from three decades in the corporate world and now spends his time volunteering with animal organizations, writing, running a book club, and taking art classes. His passion has long been in writing prose and, to that end, he has had two collections of short stories previously published— *Urban Legend* (Thistledown Press) and *The Quantum Theory of Love and Madness* (Guernica Editions). He has served as a judge for The Writer's Union of Canada's annual short fiction contest for many years and has done similar work for the humanitarian organization Ve'ahavta, judging short stories from people who have experienced homelessness. He also writes book reviews that appear in *The Ottawa Review of Books*. He has a B.Comm degree from Concordia University in Montreal and a TESL certificate from the Canadian Centre for Language and Cultural Studies (CCLCS) in Toronto.

Printed by Imprimerie Gauvin
Gatineau, Québec